Gamma Strike
Legacy War Book 8

John Walker

Copyright © 2019 John Walker

All rights reserved. No part of this publication may be reproduced, distributed, or transmitted in any form or by any means, including photocopying, recording, or other electronic or mechanical methods, without the prior written permission of the publisher, except in the case of brief quotations embodied in critical reviews and certain other noncommercial uses permitted by copyright law.

DISCLAIMER

This is a work of fiction. Names, characters, business, places, events, and incidents are either the products of the author's imagination or used in a fictitious manner. Any resemblance to actual persons, living or dead, or actual events is purely coincidental. This story contains explicit language and violence.

Blurb

An End in Sight

Four of the six Orbs have been brought together, combined in an effort to hunt down the secret base of the dreaded Tol'An terrorists. Humanity and their allies have gathered together on Earth to discuss the final attack, combining forces to bring peace to the galaxy. It is a time of hope and anticipation.

But even as the allies stand ready, they find themselves faced with a desperate enemy, one willing to do whatever it takes to win the day. As they struggle against forces outside and in, humanity must fight like never before for the stakes have never been higher. They face the utter destruction of the planet Earth...and all of humanity with it.

Prologue

Gizan Relik turned the collar of his coat up, bowing his head. A line formed to disembark the ratty passenger ship, one where the captain didn't ask any questions as long as he received cash. They arrived on a resource world, one where all the industry revolved around mining, logging, and cultivating the local wildlife for food.

He hoped to lay low there for a while, take stock of his resources before moving on to somewhere more permanent. The Pahxin government always had him on their most wanted list and now the Tol'An sought him as well. He hoped the latter's days were numbered but the former likely would never give up the hunt for him.

That made finding a safe system problematic. Gizan stuck to the fringe of society, places where a man might blend in and disappear. By doing so, he evaded the authorities and kept himself out of danger. The galaxy should've been big enough to avoid unwanted contact but that hadn't proven to be the case.

The first planet he attempted to visit, he thought would be perfect. Small population, rarely bothered by any authorities, and the Tol'An never bothered with it. Unfortunately, he stuck out in the close-knit community and their local lawman tried to apprehend him. That resulted in a murder and a stolen shuttle.

That incident taught him he needed bigger crowds to blend into, the types of people who had their own problems and didn't want to bother with someone else's. He needed hard workers, the type that pushed themselves in the morning so that by the evening, they were too exhausted to be nosey.

When he arrived on the new planet, he intended to dig in and hide. If he left one of the main camps, he'd have the opportunity to enjoy some isolation, to figure things out. A chance to sleep without worrying about being stabbed sounded nice. He hadn't been able to rest comfortably since before Ezria imprisoned him for his failure to capture the ambassadors.

The line started moving and Gizan stepped down the ramp, departing from the others as soon as he had room to do so. No one looked up from their shoes as they moved off to whatever assignment waited for them. He envied some of them, wondered what it would be like to have so little to focus on.

Gizan never had a normal life. He'd been trained by the Pahxin from a young age to be a special operative, a man capable of fighting for his people. He met Calatha Dervia during his formative years, the founder of the Tol'An, and embarked on a journey that changed him forever.

Becoming the blade of a new movement granted him power and prestige, the sort of admiration a young person craved. The killing never bothered him. His only desire was to see the will of his master done, to know that he had successfully performed his duty and forwarded the goals of his organization.

Ezria changed all that. The man seemed to understand the best way to do his job, to take the Tol'An to the next level but he proved to be petty. His understanding of sentient behavior left much to be desired. He imprisoned for small infractions, killed for others and never got his own hands dirty.

He was the worst kind of ruler, selfish and cruel. Ezria rarely made his vision clear but he acted as if it must be followed to the exclusion of all else. That was how Calatha differed. He always painted a clear image of what the future held and what it would take to get there. Others followed because they were inspired, not blindly devoted.

After imprisonment, Gizan knew he was in the wrong place. The Tol'An had gone down a path he could no longer follow. Those who worked for their new masters did so out of fear, not zeal but they couldn't tell the difference. It worked in some ways however, once the Pahxin considered them a credible threat, they needed real passion to succeed.

Beyond the passion to survive and serve.

The crowd began to thin. Gizan moved to the edge of the room, peering back at the people around him. They continued to keep their heads down, none of them so much as sparing him a glance. That suited him perfectly. It meant he could get out of there without incident. The best part was he saw no one resembling the law lingering about.

In fact, there were no weapons at all. That part seemed odd though even Gizan traveled with only a pair of blades for self-defense. The types of transports he hopped on didn't check people but open firearms weren't allowed onboard. He'd seen what happened to one spacer who tried to bring a massive pistol with him.

They tossed him out and he had to wait for the next ship.

The spaceport was a fabricated complex with three landing pads. The steepled roof overhead provided some cover from the elements. A dirt path led away from the structure into a town of square buildings, each one made of metal and covered in moss. People conducted business down there, milling about.

Apparently, they'd arrived near quitting time for the average worker in that region. That suited Gizan. He blended in with a crowd that headed toward the town, keeping his head down as he walked. People bumped into him to the left and right but he'd become accustomed to being in such close proximity to strangers.

Still, he remained cautious, maintaining his situational awareness. Someone joined their ranks the moment the crowd passed them, two men who were far too clean to be average workers. The fact they hurried to catch up bothered Gizan but he didn't dare to look back over his shoulder at them. No one else showed signs of curiosity. He couldn't either.

Voices muttered comments behind him, people saying *excuse me* here and there. He figured the two people must've been trying to shove their way to the front of the group but why bother? They were moving at a brisk pace. Rushing wouldn't get them there too much further and the ground was slick anyway.

A man would fall if he moved too fast.

They reached the bottom of the hill. Gizan glanced over his shoulder, noting the two men staring directly at him. *How did they find me?* The thought infuriated him. He had been careful. Cash only, using destitute captains and ships on the verge of falling apart. The fringes of society had become his home and yet, here he was faced with another attack.

Worse, he couldn't tell if they were Pahxin authorities or Tol'An murderers. Their allegiance only mattered when it came to how fast they could call in reinforcements. The former would have access to a ship which could travel freely. It might've even been in orbit already. The latter needed to remain stealthy.

They weren't in control of the universe yet.

Gizan picked up the pace, pushing to the front of the group. Once there, he broke away, moving for the first building on his left. It appeared to be a general store, one that sold tools and clothing. He entered the thirty by thirty space. Shovels sat on the wall nearest him and he grabbed one, hefting the weight in his hands.

Clothing racks took up the center of the space. Smaller tools climbed up the wall on the right. A counter where people could transact business sat opposite the door and a Pahxin woman manned it. She eyed him suspiciously and when he turned in her direction, she cleared her throat.

"Can I help you?" She asked.

"No one can," Gizan replied. He turned his attention to the door as two shadows darkened the entry. He held the shovel at the ready. The first of his pursuers stepped into the room and he swung high, catching the man in the face with flat metal. A high-pitched metallic ding rang out as the man's feet flew out from under him and he landed on his back.

His friend reached into his jacket. Gizan stabbed him with the pointy end of his spade, driving him into the wall. Pressing all of his weight into the attack, he felt the shovel meet bone through the gut. Blood burst from the victim's mouth, his eyes closed in tight pain a few moments before he slumped, dead.

The woman screamed. A hand grabbed Gizan's foot. He turned to look at the man on the ground, flailing about with his eyes rolling back in his skull. "We found you …" he muttered. "Lord Ezria has put … a price … you are a traitor! A filthy … miserable … traitor. You're going to die. It's only a matter of time."

"Tol'An then." Gizan ripped his makeshift weapon free and pressed it to the man's throat. "I owe you thanks. It seems that escape was not an option after all. I appreciate you making that abundantly clear."

"No …" The man flailed his arms again. "Please … I was only …"

Gizan stomped on the shovel, feeling it cut deep into the man's neck. The body stiffened then flopped. "Following orders?" He asked. "Yes, I'm sure we've all used that excuse from time to time. It doesn't save anyone. This is all you would've had to look forward to. Death for a failure. Regardless of how many successes you returned."

He turned to the woman who stared at him with wide-eyed horror. She trembled behind the counter, petrified. "I ... please ..." She held up her hands. "I don't have any idea who you are. I won't tell anyone. Just ... don't hurt me. Please, don't."

"I won't." Gizan approached the counter. He dropped some cash, tapping it three times. "For the shovel. I doubt anyone will want to buy that one. I included some extra to make up for the inconvenience. I know it won't help erase what you had to see but I assure you, those men deserved what they got."

"I'm sure I don't know."

"No. But when your authorities check them, they'll find they are terrorists working for the Tol'An." Gizan knew he didn't have any time. He needed to return to the port, to force the captain to get him out of there. The law would be interested in putting the man away who savagely murdered two people with a digging implement. "Good luck ... and again, I'm sorry."

Gizan stepped outside, walking calmly back the way he came up the hill. Everyone continued to mind their own business but he knew that discipline was about to break down. Once they knew they had a murderer to contend with, they would all get in on the gossip. Until someone was caught, safety would be in question.

He'd seen the same in several places all over the galaxy. The moment routine broke, those living in its embrace tended to panic. Unfortunately for those living in the immediate area, they would not get any closure. The killer wasn't going to be brought to justice and so they would be left to wonder.

Gizan boarded the ship again, heading to the small bridge. He drew one of his concealed blades, creeping silently along the metal grated floor. The doors were open ahead and he saw a lone man sitting in the pilot's seat, counting money. An open metal box sat nearby, stacks of cash haphazardly lying inside.

Pressing the blade against the man's neck, Gizan leaned in close. He could smell sweat and fear on the man, body odor from days aboard without washing. "I'm afraid I need your help again, captain. What is your name?"

"Er … um …" The man stiffened but kept his hands still. "Rythi. I'm Captain Rythi. There's no need for the weapon."

"I can't be sure about that but I'm pleased to meet you. We have somewhere to go but I won't be able to pay you, not right away. It's a rather urgent request as well so I'll give you the coordinates after we've launched. I'm sure you understand. You've likely had to leave many places quickly."

"What do you want?"

"We need to go. I've got a destination. Upon arrival, you'll be handsomely rewarded but it will be dangerous."

"How handsomely?"

Gizan smiled at the greed in Rythi's voice. "Whatever legal troubles have you working the fringe lanes will be over."

"How dangerous?"

"Now you're worried about that?" Gizan drew back. "Have you heard of the Tol'An?"

"Who hasn't? Those maniacs have made it hard for honest traders in some parts of the galaxy." Rythi shook his head. "Haven't hit me yet. I've stayed out of their way."

"Then to answer your question, we'll be stepping directly in their way ... and taking care of them once and for all." Gizan patted his shoulder. "Look on the bright side. You'll be hailed as a hero. The man who assisted in the downfall of the greatest terrorist organization to plague the galaxy."

"And you can do that?"

Gizan's eyes flashed. "I *will* do it."

Chapter 1

Cassandra Alexander stared out the window of the descending shuttle, peering at the empty landscape. Gamma Alpha was situated on the left and the supporting town only a couple miles away but to her right, mountains and forest stretched out as far as the eye could see.

The terrain offered a fantastic cover for the force that attacked them while they transported the Orb. That had been before they secured two more. Intelligence called the organization an Earth-based terrorist organization but they seemed far too organized for that. In Cassie's mind, she considered them a hostile militia at least.

Army seemed more appropriate. Someone paid big to get them into position, to gather the intelligence of just when to attack. Christina Dawson had been assigned to investigate but no report made it to the Gnosis yet. Of course, they had only just arrived in orbit and were sending down their final prize: the last Orb known to be in the wild.

Completing the last mission took a toll on the men. Several marines died, including an entire team. A Pahxin technical crew also lost their lives not to mention countless scavengers, raiders, pirates and Tol'An operatives. She thought back on the report she wrote for the AIA and shivered.

The previous culture attempted to pacify their population, to take care of rampant crime and chaos. Instead, they made something deadly and it ended their entire race, destroying their planet in the process. Only a space station survived and with it, the technology which continued to thrive and kill anyone who visited.

How many other booby traps are out there waiting to be discovered by an unsuspecting crew? Cassie didn't want to think too much about it. When they finished the war with the Tol'An, she planned on offering a recommendation to the AIA that a crew be assigned to travel about, looking for those types of threats to quell them.

Knowing my luck, they'll assign me to that team. Cassie wasn't sure what she wanted to do when it all ended. She had been assigned to the Gnosis as a specialist on Orb technology and ended up part of the crew. They accepted her as one of their own but the things she'd done, the trials she endured went above and beyond the call of duty.

Retirement wasn't an option, not at her age but there had to be something else she could do with herself that didn't involve running such risky operations. Christina had survived years of fieldwork and seemed okay. Then again, she never had a psychic connection with an Orb before.

And Cassie managed to do it several times. Not to mention the encounters out in the middle of nowhere with ancient cultures all lost to the seas of time. Their legacies tended to be deadly, broken machinery or simply monotonous automation left to continue protocols without sentient guidance.

Captain Desmond Bradford seemed to believe they would become explorers when the conflict was over, that they would finally fulfill the destiny the ship had been built for in the first place. Cassie wanted to be cautiously optimistic but the Tol'An represented only one threat they faced in the cosmos.

The Kalrawv Group, vicious corporate stooges bent on exploiting alien relics, remained in effect. Their public face couldn't be holding up after the things they'd done but Cassie knew how big businesses operated. They were slippery and knew the laws sometimes better than those who made them.

They would remain out there, causing trouble for the foreseeable future.

Then there were the raiders and pirates. They represented a varying degree of danger depending on how well funded they were. Whoever traveled beyond Earth's borders would need to contend with them as well, defending themselves from those types of threats no matter where they went.

Even without a boogeyman, the universe would remain a scary place. The threat itself would be harder to identify, but it would be there. Until the next group rose up with ideas of conquest and subjugation. Such things were inevitable. Earth's own history proved it time and again.

Someone always believed they knew better than the current ruling party and then, the seeds of rebellion would sprout.

I'm feeling particularly cynical today. Cassie sighed and turned to her tablet, looking over the meetings she had planned for the day. Several people wanted her time, from Doctor Harper's crew to her own leadership to the admiral and even ... The last entry gave her pause. Her sister arrived at Gamma Alpha and wanted to see her.

That's a surprise. Tammy had been in college when Cassie joined the Gnosis crew. They hadn't spoken in all that time and rarely wrote. *Why would she come here? What could she possibly need?* The fact her own family had to schedule time to talk spoke of how busy her schedule was.

Cassie accepted all the meeting requests and flipped through her messages. Beaumont Dulain sent her three separate requests to ensure she would be at their meeting. She replied to him that she would as soon as she saw the Orb secured. Four marines sat around her, each in their power armor to escort the device to its new home.

What did he expect me to do? Skip it? Sometimes, she wondered if Dulain knew he was in charge. Then she thought about how many agents must've skipped key meetings with their superiors to warrant his insistent curiosity. Christina had a different relationship with the man, the type that involved speaking far more plainly than Cassie ever would've.

Of course, they'd worked together for years so perhaps they paved the way for frank conversation. Cassie saw Dulain exactly three times in person before she joined the Gnosis and each of those were during large meetings with her entire department present. The first time they met in private, she'd been scared out of her mind.

Spending time with him became far easier. He'd become demystified, shown to be a regular person for the most part. His methods left something to be desired in her mind, especially since he didn't act like the most professional individual. Cassie felt they could be more open with their allies. Dulain wanted them to play things close to the chest.

This included her interactions with the Gnosis crew. Dulain gave her all sorts of powers she had yet to exercise, including the ability to take command should the need arise. Fortunately, she'd never felt it necessary, never pushed Captain Bradford with the authority. In fact, she told him about it.

Cassie wanted to ensure a positive relationship remained between her and the people she relied on to keep her alive. Giving them cause to forsake her for any reason seemed stupid. They didn't have any particular allegiance to her, nothing beyond the camaraderie forged from working together.

The last thing she needed was to bust out a secret during a stressful situation and risk an argument at a critical moment. She'd seen how quickly choices had to be made to preserve the lives of everyone on board the Gnosis. Anything that interrupted that process could have been fatal.

Everyone had a job for a reason and they were entrusted to do it properly. That included Captain Bradford. Whether Dulain liked it or not, the man was in charge for a reason. He had exhibited the necessary traits to act as a leader, a person who knew what was best for the mission he'd been given.

If Dulain wanted to alter the parameters, he should've gone through proper channels. Cassie believed that Bradford would've done whatever the AIA wanted providing their goals were written into the operational requirements. Of course, the intelligence agency wanted to remain secretive so they played games.

"Landing in less than five minutes," the pilot spoke up. "Guards are on hand to escort the Orb in. Be on your guards, folks. The base is on yellow status. They sound pretty stressed down there."

Great, so they're worried about another attack. Cassie sighed. She tried to dial up Christina, to see if she might establish a com with the woman. It pinged six times before connecting.

"Cassie?" Christina's voice came in loud and clear. "Welcome back! Are you onboard the shuttle coming down?"

"Thanks, I am," Cassie replied. "Are you on security detail?"

"No, I'm fully invested in taking care of our local trouble," Christina said. "We had a breakthrough. I'm pretty sure we know where the enemy's hanging out but the real traitor, that's who I'm after. Do you have any news you'd like to share on that front? We're pouring through roughly seven hundred personnel files so if you can fast-track us, that would be great."

"I'm afraid not. We were up to our ears in work while we were gone. You won't even believe what happened. In any event, we're about to touchdown and I wanted to see if you'd be there when we landed."

"So you got the Orb then?"

Cassie smiled. "We sure did ... though ..." She sighed. "It wasn't entirely easy. And we paid a big price for it. Still, it's here right? That's all that matters."

"No," Christina said. "Maybe I believed that when I was young, but it's hard to say the ends justify the means. Sometimes, they don't. Even when they do, there's not much comfort to be had in losing lives for it. I started thinking of it as lost potential ... the chance for people to have families, grow old, made the world a better place ... probably not super healthy."

"Not for your state of mind." Cassie looked outside again. The ground grew ever closer. "I'm assuming I'll get a chance to see you in some meeting or other, right? Dulain isn't going to keep you sequestered away the whole time I'm here, right?"

"You think you're leaving again soon?"

"Once they use the four Orbs to find the last two, we'll have the location of the Tol'An," Cassie explained. "And yeah, between us and the Pahxin, I'm pretty sure we're going to go in and finish them off. Don't you think?"

"I wouldn't be surprised if the Gnosis sits that out," Christina replied. "After all, it's not a warship. A bunch of battles doesn't change that fact. Yeah, you've done amazing but I think the brass might want to preserve what we've got left. Don't quote me on any of that though. I'm just a grunt doing a job."

"Yeah, I'm sure you haven't been considered that for years." Cassie shook her head. "Anyway, we'll see. And I'm sure we'll talk soon. Thanks for picking up. Cassandra out." She tapped her tablet and braced herself for the final approach. As the landing gear deployed, the deck rumbled for a moment just seconds before the retro rockets kicked in.

The ship jostled about as they made the final descent. Landing gear sunk as it connected with the tarmac. Hydraulics hissed around them and the marines rose in an instant, stamping to the door. Cassie disengaged her safety belt and stood back, allowing them to open the ramp and storm out.

They secured the area, met up with the escorts, and planned their path to get the payload to where it belonged. Cassie followed along, drawing a deep breath of Earth air. It felt nice to be back, even if it meant throwing herself into a busy schedule of meetings and conversations.

And seeing Tammy, Cassie thought. *The strangest and possibly hardest part of all this. I hope everything's okay. The last thing I want is a little family drama just before we head out to save the galaxy.*

***

Captain Desmond Bradford remained on the bridge of the Gnosis, overseeing the arrival of tech crews from Earth. Preparation for the final fight with the Tol'An began the second they arrived back in system, including some tweaks to the weapons systems, defenses, and reactor. The hope was to get two shots off before the generators had to recharge.

Admiral Reach contacted him the moment they left hyperspace as if he'd been sitting on the com with a constant ping heading their way. The eagerness was not one-sided. Desmond looked forward to giving them the good news. Even with the number of losses they experienced, their success pushed them one step closer toward finishing the war.

The key was whether or not the four orbs would provide them the means to find the final two. If they could do that, then the attack on the Tol'An headquarters would commence. The full might of the Pahxin and Earth's own ship would swoop down upon them. With such an overwhelming force, the fight should've been single sided.

Desmond worried more about the Kalrawv Group than the Tol'An. They seemed to be a real threat, one that operated under the noses of the authorities. Of course, the law couldn't be everywhere and it was clear by the way the Pahxin treated them during one of their earlier operations that they didn't enjoy any sort of special status.

He hoped his people would push hard to have the organization investigated properly once the Tol'An were contended with. They shouldn't be allowed to roam the galaxy, exploiting resources for their own gain at any time. He found it reprehensible, especially since they had no qualms about kidnapping people to complete their projects.

Even the people who willingly worked for them didn't make out all that great. Those people were little more than indentured servants, making low wages in terrible conditions. He was surprised they weren't forced to use corporate vouchers for their food and equipment, made to pay for their rooms.

Commander Vincent Bowman joined him on the bridge, sitting heavily in the chair beside him. The blond man rubbed his eyes before speaking. "I've been to engineering. They're all ready for the techs to show up. Everything's clean at least. Hangar bay's all cleared out. Replacement fighters will be ready in a couple hours."

"Great news," Desmond said. "Now, let's hope they figure out where we're going fast. I don't want to sit around here any longer than we have to."

"What did Reach have to say?"

Desmond shrugged. "He's anxious but there's nothing any of us can do to hurry things along. So I told him we'd do what we could with the ship while Doctor Harper's team works with the Orbs. Keep us all busy this way *and* we don't have to be down there to see the poor man pace a hole in his floor."

Vincent smirked. "We need to get these techies aboard so our crew can get some rest. That last one … we can't expect them to jump right back in. We need a day, three would be better. Especially for the marines. They took it hard in that last run. And our pilots definitely need some downtime."

"We've been pushing hard, I agree." Desmond leaned forward and rubbed his face. "I just don't know how long it'll be before we have to go. It could happen fast. And if it does, we can't have our people all over the place. They need to be in close proximity, ready to get back to the Gnosis at a moment's notice."

"Then to Gamma Alpha at least," Vincent said. "We'll have shuttles on standby but I'm telling you, these guys have given us over a hundred percent. They need to recharge."

Desmond nodded. "Okay, I agree. Set up a schedule. Prioritize the marines and pilots. And make sure you take some time yourself. I'm sure you and Cassie can find a couple minutes to hang out together."

Vincent's cheeks turned red. "Yeah, well ... things might be getting a little serious you know?" He shrugged. "At least, I'm hoping so. Wouldn't hurt my feelings at least."

"Careful," Desmond said. "Intelligence agents might not be the best choice for dating."

"I don't think she's going to stick with it." Vincent shook his head. "Wouldn't surprise me if she got out as soon as this is over."

"I've met her type. They don't quit. This is what she's trained for and it's what she's going to do until they kick her out. Hell, I bet she ends up with Dulain's job at some point. She's got better ethics than he does at least. Might be the best thing that ever happened to the AIA, to be honest."

"You know what she's been through," Vincent replied. "All that crap with getting *into* the Orb? That's enough to shake anyone."

"Yes ..." Desmond nodded. "But she's also been through too much to throw in the towel. I'm telling you, she's got ambition. And once this is over and she can take a minute to breathe, she's going to be all in. Just be ready. If things get serious, you might end up with a career politician on your hands. Besides, I thought you wanted a command."

"I do ... I did." Vincent sighed. "All the things we've seen have made me second guess my calling, I suppose. Like you say, maybe when things are all over I'll have a change of heart. Right now ... right now, I'm just tired." He smirked. "Don't get me wrong, I'm all in to see this through. But afterward, I'm hoping for some real leave."

"If all goes according to plan," Desmond said, "shouldn't be a problem." His com went off and he established the connection. "Captain Bradford."

"Hey, it's Cassie. Orb's secure. They're connecting them up to the network right now. ETA two hours."

"Were your ears burning?" Desmond asked, glancing at Vincent.

"Sir?" Cassie paused. "Oh. I'm doing alright if that was the topic of conversation."

"Nah. Just gossiping up here. Do we need to do anything to help?"

"No, Doctor Harper's team is on it. I'm going to meetings until they're ready to try some things then I'll throw myself into that for a bit. I've decided I'll be stopping at seventeen-hundred though. Even if these guys plan on going all night, I'd like to get a decent night of rest on our first day back."

"I endorse that decision." Desmond pursed his lips. "Vincent will be on his way down in the next half hour if you need him for anything. Feel free to link up with his com. He shouldn't have anything scheduled either since it was a bit spontaneous. I'm sure he has a unique perspective that could come in handy with the Orbs."

"Oh …" Cassie sounded surprised and a touch relieved. "That would be lovely. Sometimes, these folks forget what we've done. It's nice to have backup when explaining our missions."

"Then that works perfectly. Talk to you soon, Cassie. Desmond out." He turned to Vincent. "You're welcome."

"Sir, I haven't put together the leave schedule. I've got a dozen things to take care of."

"Don't worry about it. I can make a schedule. Besides, you were one of the people who needed leave, remember?"

"What about you?"

Desmond chuckled. "The fact I'm not sitting in Admiral Reach's office is vacation enough for me right now. Seriously, get out of here. Take a shuttle down and spend some time with that woman. Maybe I'm wrong about her and if I am, then you can't ignore any opportunity. You know what I mean?"

"I do … thank you." Vincent went to the elevator and paused. "You're absolutely sure?"

"I'm about to change my mind," Desmond teased. "Get out of here, Commander."

Once Vincent left, Desmond turned back to his terminal. Reports came in from engineering. Tech crews had arrived and were starting in on the upgrades. Replacement ships were being stowed and checked over to ensure they were safe. Medical moved injured crew down to the surface.

They didn't have an ETA on when the upgrades would be completed but none of the proposals looked particularly complicated. He brought up the personnel roster, scheduling leave for the crew. The tricky part was finding enough shuttles to ferry them back and forth in a timely fashion.

Ground control offered a solution, providing him with an additional three shuttles to get his people down there. An hour later, Desmond leaned back in his chair and stretched his arms. That task completed, he wasn't sure what else to do but be available. He went through every alert, saw they were for different section chiefs, and settled in for a boring few hours.

Better than exciting, Desmond thought. *Maybe this is all the rest I need.* There was something to be said about quiet time on the bridge. No one shooting at them, no one being shot on some alien planet surface. Just the curve of the Earth beyond the view screen and the quiet activities of Deacon on the helm.

It had been the first time he did not have to immediately rush back to Gamma Alpha for briefings and meetings, conversations and other engagements. Much like his advice given to Vincent, he decided he'd take what pleasure he could from the moment. He ordered up some coffee, planning to enjoy the peace and quiet. While it lasted.

***

Beaumont Dulain found himself running around like he'd been caught on fire. So many different departments wanted his attention, he started to feel like he'd taken a demotion. Those directly beneath him were just as busy, just as consistently occupied with meetings and briefings. The AIA had never been tapped so hard in the past.

With the end of the Tol'An drawing near, the Pahxin intelligence community brought a full department to Earth. Their aim was to assist with deciphering any information drawn from the extra Orbs. Their expertise proved invaluable in regular espionage as well. They brought back information from all parts of the galaxy as spies hunted for clues.

One, in particular, involved a high-level breach in Tol'An ranks. Dulain just finished a briefing where one of the Pahxin told them that a key member of the terrorist elite had left gone AWOL, departing the organization. The deserter found himself pursued by the law as well as his former comrades.

The Pahxin government hoped to enlist him for aid against the Tol'An. He undoubtedly knew a great deal about their infrastructure, including the location of their headquarters. Unfortunately, he didn't allow anyone to talk to him, turning violent upon each confrontation. He'd left a trail of bodies from the Kalrawv mining operation to outposts on the fringe.

Dulain learned more about the Tol'An in general, about their original founder Calatha Dervia. He'd been a thoughtful, peaceful politician who radicalized after his family died. He originally envisioned his new group to be a lawful group meant to bring about change to society, to teach values which would ultimately assuage crime.

He quickly found his fellows were not prepared to give up so many freedoms for his dream and took his followers off world. Most of them were fanatics, zealots who suffered in a similar manner. Intelligence suggested Calatha died at some point and one of his faithful took over. A change in tactics was their first clue.

Initially, the Tol'An used guerrilla tactics, hitting hard and leaving before a proper response could be leveraged. After Calatha, they adopted a military mindset, meaning open engagements. Some of them were successful, especially after they managed to convert several high-ranking military officials.

Others proved disastrous as poor leaders were given charge of complex operations. The question Dulain had was why did the Tol'An have so many people working for them? What allure did they have to adopt such a following? Especially with their current leadership proving to be little more than a power crazed maniac.

At least that's how the reports painted him. Ultimately, it wouldn't matter. The combined force of Earth and the Pahxin would be down on their organization soon enough and the threat of the terrorist group would be mostly over. Statistics showed that at least thirty percent of their forces would remain combat effective elsewhere in the galaxy.

Leaderless and without supply, they would become raiders and pirates. Dulain proposed a special unit to hunt them down, an organization that could persist after the threat had been neutralized for other such issues. The reports from the Gnosis proved criminals were just as much of a problem as the more overt groups.

His Pahxin counterparts agreed and they insisted they would take the suggestion to their government. Dulain went above his authority by offering up an Earth ship to join that group, though they had yet to build it. He wanted in on, to ensure humanity held representation in any capacity possible.

Dulain met with his boss early that morning. Their goal was to go over some options of who they planned on recommending for an ambassador position with the Pahxin. He was surprised to see his own name on the list and quickly removed himself. They would be suspicious of his presence on the planet.

After all, he'd done with them, they would have to assume he was spying on them. No amount of talking them down would prove otherwise. They needed a man or woman without ties to the intelligence community. He recommended Admiral Reach. The man already proved himself to them several times. He exemplified human integrity.

Whether or not Reach wanted to live on an alien world was another matter entirely.

All of that came about and Dulain barely had an opportunity to speak with Christina about her investigation. He knew that she was tapping military resources while examining every personnel record on Gamma Alpha but beyond that, he had a pile of reports he hadn't read. At least she seemed to be effective but he wouldn't know until they talked.

The human insurrectionists needed to be taken out of the equation as soon as possible. They held the advantage of anonymity, meaning their operations could take place at any time without warning. Christina managed to grab considerable intel from them. If the military didn't lay into something soon, Dulain would be surprised.

Then finally, a fourth Orb had been delivered to Earth. He couldn't wait to speak to Doctor Harper and her people. They hadn't even been able to fully explore the benefit of having three of the devices but now, with four of them he anticipated great things. Doctor Thayne Rindala of the Pahxin stated they never had so many in one place.

This gave them both a major advantage and a dilemma. The Pahxin allowed them to keep the devices because of the collective expertise on the planet surrounding the technology. But other organizations may have seen them as a prize. For this reason, the Pahxin stationed three battleships around Earth to help keep them safe.

Their presence made some of the military nervous. If relations broke down, nothing would stop them from trashing the planet and taking whatever they wanted. Dulain used to share their concerns but after working closely with them, he changed his tune. They were a people with integrity and would use diplomacy before violence.

The second problem that worried authorities came down to the destructive power of the Orbs. As an energy source, it was a well-known fact they carried the capability to annihilate large sections of any planet they happened to be stationed on. Doctor Harper helpfully provided the figures to her superiors who in turn terrified the military.

With all four Orbs in one place, they were capable of destroying the planet. Technically, the majority of the continent would be decimated along with a large chunk that would send the rest of the world into a cataclysmic event. Nothing would survive. The sun itself exploding wouldn't do the job much better.

This meant Reach's team had to justify keeping the devices together for their research, to show that the risk was worth the reward. Dulain attempted to help but he didn't have any data to backup his belief. Some suggested they move the devices off-world, to find a place that wouldn't matter if explode.

Timing prevented that discussion from going too far. They needed to find the Tol'An and finish them off. Doing so required the Orbs. Afterward, Dulain figured the Pahxin would want theirs back. Harper proved that they could be used as instantaneous communication devices. This meant that at one time there were likely six cultures cooperating throughout the galaxy.

The question of what happened to them had been partially answered by Cassandra Alexander when she psychically connected with one of the Orbs on the way back from their first mission. Technology gone wild brought about a terrifying end to multiple systems. A computer virus that must've gone dormant or no longer found perch in modern equipment.

Dulain privately looked forward to bringing all six of the Orbs together, to see if that unlocked something special. He assumed it would. The ones who could build such wonders intrigued him. He wanted to know more. That was the exploration he found himself most invested in. Not discovering new worlds, but the secrets of the past.

Where had those people gone? So far, the Gnosis encountered a planet where the inhabitants copied their minds into computers and another where the population mutated into tribal, cannibal beasts. Had the designers of the Orbs suffered a similar fate? Or was this their legacy, the last vestige of their contribution to the galaxy?

A message popped up on his tablet, indicating Cassie had arrived well over an hour earlier. He'd wanted to be there when she arrived, to talk about their previous mission and see the final Orb himself. He canceled his next two meetings, asking them to reschedule before rushing off to the tech lab.

Gamma Alpha became Dulain's new home. When things settled down, he committed to visiting his house on the west coast of North America. Vacation seemed like a dirty word but if he didn't get some downtime in, he knew he'd lose his edge. Well, more than half the people at the base were in the same boat.

What this meant was that Dulain rarely found time to escape the constant barrage of requests. He'd return to his quarters only to find people waiting for him with questions or concerns. Privacy became a luxury he no longer enjoyed. He doubted he would know what to do with it if he got it.

Cassie just stepped out of the lab when he arrived.

"What's going on?" Dulain asked. "Have they hooked them up?"

"They're working on it," Cassie replied. "Won't be long before they're able to run some tests. Then it's up to Gil and me to see what we can come up with."

"The device still isn't ready? The one that you guys discovered on your trip?"

Cassie shook her head. "Not yet. They've fabricated the parts but putting it together has been challenging ... at least in a way that the power source doesn't burn out instantly. They complained about cooling but I backed out of the conversation, to be honest."

"I understand." Dulain frowned, then realized he'd gone straight business mode. "I'm sorry, how're you doing? How was the last mission? I haven't had a chance to read your report yet."

"I'm fine," Cassie replied, "but the mission was rough. I'll let you read about it. Suffice to say, a lot of people died to bring us back this Orb."

"Risk and reward," Dulain grumbled. "I used to be able to talk about that with far less cynicism but lately, I've been losing my stomach for it. Christina's had a few breakthroughs. I haven't kept up with her reports either but I feel certain she's close. She's got a new agent who's eager to make a name for himself."

"I talked to her on the way down," Cassie replied. "They are close."

"Great! So ..." Dulain clapped his hands. "Do you want lunch? I'd be happy to get you out of the limelight for a while so you can enjoy some downtime with food. If that's on the agenda."

"I can't. I've got plans with Commander Bowman."

Dulain lifted his brows. "Really. So that's persisting. You guys ... making a go of it."

"We have been," Cassie replied. She lifted her chin. "I don't think it's a problem ..."

"No, not at all. It certainly hasn't cut into your effectiveness at all." Dulain smiled. "I'm happy for you honestly. In the middle of all this madness, it's hard to remember that we're still people. Connections are important. We need them. I'm glad you found one on this trip, especially since we thought those military types would've shunned you for being AIA."

"I'd like to think I was too charming for all that." Cassie smiled this time. "That was a serious joke. I've got about as much charm as an ant line at a picnic. I don't know what Vincent ... Commander Bowman sees in me, to be honest. I went aboard all business and ... well ... this is what came about."

"I find it funny," Dulain said, "that you know so much about an alien technology but so little about how relationships work. Didn't you date in school? Secondary, I mean. Not at AIA training."

"No ... not really. I ..." Cassie shrugged. "I was focused."

"To the exclusion of normalcy." Dulain patted her shoulder. "Anyway, connections happen when you're least expecting and always when you're *not* looking for them. I doubt your commander thought he'd end up like this when he boarded the Gnosis. Especially when the war with the Tol'An broke out."

"Maybe so." Cassie checked her tablet. "Sorry, I've got to go …"

"Go ahead." Dulain waved his hand down the hall. "I'm going to visit with Doctor Harper and see what trouble I can get into with the tech lab. Have fun. Relax a little bit. Until they've got these things talking, there's no reason for you to come back. Consider that an order from your superior, huh?"

"Thank you." Cassie rushed off down the hall. Dulain watched her go, letting out a sigh. When he first met her, he thought she might be too earnest for the work they were assigning her. She remained too squeaky clean for some AIA work but it ended up making her good at working with the Gnosis crew.

Reports spoke highly of her. Captain Bradford gave excellent ratings for her performance. Christina enjoyed working with her when they worked out security detail for transporting the two Orbs in one of their operations. By all rights, Dulain felt like he'd made the right call elevating her to senior agent level.

Depending on how she did in the next operation, she may well be able to write her own ticket. Politics weren't out of the question. She'd already attracted the eye of several key personnel high up in different government organizations. Dulain talked about her whenever he could. She was his benevolent eye, watching the military situation unfold.

He half thought his superiors might try to replace him with someone like her. If that was the case, he wouldn't feel too bad. Especially after everything he'd been through lately. The bureaucracy was starting to wear him down and that said a lot considering how much of it he himself put in place.

Chapter 2

Christina sat with Sandoval Essex, the fresh agent who she allied herself with for her current investigation. He'd proven to be a tireless worker but even their combined efforts were making slow work of diving into the various personnel files. They couldn't lock the base down after the assault, not while keeping it running effectively.

So that meant a lot of people came and went and any one of them could've been Red Corsair, the traitor that sold out the timing for transporting the Orbs. No one had any illusions that such a person was done. They would strike again. Whether that meant another open assault or something subtle, that remained to be seen.

Essex felt as if they narrowed the list of potential suspects down to twenty. That still seemed like a lot. Only five of them were currently in Gamma Alpha. The others remained at whatever post took them away in the first place. They were singled out because they had protracted contact with various Pahxin agents.

Christina hesitated to call upon her Pahxin counterparts. She worried about who to pick, who to trust. Unfortunately, they wouldn't have a choice for long. A Tol'An agent had infiltrated the ranks of their allies and if they didn't root that individual out, they could just develop another asset.

"You know …" Christina turned to Essex. "I was just thinking. If we talked to the Pahxin, if we rooted out their traitor, we might find our own. Depending on their interrogation techniques, that is. We might at least eliminate a few options. This is a lot of people to go through. Hell, we practically need to interview them all."

"But if we tip off the agent …"

Christina waved her hand at him. "Yes, I know. I thought of that too but at some point, we're not going to have a choice. They have to be brought in."

"After we know who they should finger," Essex pointed out.

His thinking was sound but she worried about what other damage the person might be doing. No one was specifically seeking them out. Christina didn't have access to Pahxin records. If someone was causing trouble, their own people needed to be involved to catch them. Or they'd have to hack into their systems, which would *not* go over well.

Dulain hadn't been reading her reports. If he had, he would've visited them to complain. Christina would've welcomed the opportunity to requisition more agents. She already checked the pool and everyone stationed at Gamma Alpha was fully tapped out. No one could help because everything was a priority one project.

At some point, they'd have to invent a new classification to put them in some semblance of order true order.

"Let's set up the interviews." Christina rubbed her eyes. "We'll have to find a way to make it sound positive. Not like interrogations. I'm not against spooking them, but at the same time, we have to be careful. God knows what they'll be willing to do if they think they're about to be caught."

"I'll section them out," Essex said. "There are a few that know one another so we can get them to them relatively at the same time. The others are isolated from this list. Do you think we can get through them all today? I'm guessing they're all pretty busy. Their section leads will be pissed."

"Don't really care about their opinions," Christina replied. "I'll trump their authority easily enough. As far as how quickly we can get through them, we don't have a choice. If we don't pound through the entire list in short order, it'll leak we're asking questions. The person we're after will be warned."

"We might want to have lunch first then." Essex winked when Christina looked at him. She laughed despite the stress of the situation. "Just sayin'. If we're going to be that busy, I'm going to need some chow in me first. Don't want to slip up because I'm craving a damn sandwich."

"You're right. Go for it. I've got something here. I'll try to catch up with Dulain about all of this and prepare him for the shit storm of complaints he's about to receive." Christina rolled her eyes. "Not that he's reading his mail anyway. Chances are he'd just ignore those too. Must be a nice way to live ... nice or insanely stressful."

Essex patted her on the shoulder on his way by. He'd become a lot more familiar since they spent hours in the same room together. She would've preferred him to keep his hands to himself but wasn't going to make a stink about it. Not when they still had many more hours ahead of them.

Christina grabbed a sandwich from her bag and nibbled on it, staring at the photos of each of their suspects. The images started to blur together right along with the words. She hoped the interrogation turned something up. Of the twenty people they found, none of them booked an obvious trip to North Africa.

Whether they'd gone to the mountain base Christina identified and raided was another matter entirely. There was no way to know unless they would've booked a flight. She didn't see any reason for the traitor to visit the place. It was a way station, a place to store supplies and prep ops, not necessarily to stay long term.

The door opened. Christina didn't look up. "That was fast. Was there no line at the cafeteria?"

"Not sure what you're talking about," Dulain said. "Is that where your partner in crime is right now?"

"Yeah, he decided we should eat before interrogating a bunch of people." Christina turned to him. "You've been a hard person to get a hold of."

"You know how it goes. We have four Orbs here now. Security just tightened. Another seventy marines are stationed here now. Half of them have power armor. It's pretty incredible. Military services pulled them together fast. I'm impressed." Dulain shrugged. "In any event, they're working through the process of connecting them."

"So everyone's chomping at the bit to see what happens," Christina said. "And whether or not we can go hit the Tol'An."

Dulain nodded. "We've practically got the Pahxin on speed dial for the moment we know where to hit. They're committing quite the fleet to the endeavor. Admiral Reach privately told me he's leery about sending the Gnosis but feels like he has to. If we're not represented … I'm with him on both sentiments."

"They're capable enough," Christina replied. "Besides, there's no way those terrorist bastards are going to stand up to a full-scale assault and we both know that. It'll be a sweep and clear."

"Maybe. But I can't quite get a bad feeling out of my gut." Dulain shrugged. "They seem like the type to do something crazy. Like, blow up one of the Orbs to stop us." He held up his hand as if to stave off an argument. "Seriously speaking, why wouldn't they? If they were about to be utterly destroyed, removed from the galaxy, what's to stop them?"

"The knowhow," Christina said. "Just get in there before they can initiate anything like that. Here's the thing, they haven't prepped it to blow on their own planet. That would be insane. They'd have to go through the whole process." She paused. "Maybe that's a point to consider. Get people down there and take those before it goes south."

"Ah, as in raid the planet as quickly as possible while ships engage above orbit." Dulain nodded. "I like it. That's a great point. Well done."

Christina shrugged. "At least I've got one good idea. This investigation is mired in too much data. And I have no idea when or if these pricks are going to try to hit us again. All I can say is a bona fide maybe. Did they blow their wad on the Gamma Alpha assault? No. That's certain because we saw their forces in the mountain."

"Okay, so they're definitely still out there. Do you want the military to hit them at that base?"

"I'm afraid they'll have already left." Christina sighed. "Why wouldn't they? We escaped. They don't know who we work for so if they have any intelligence at all, they're assuming we're with some government agency. If they stay, they're digging in for an assault, preparing themselves for a fight. Which means our guys would have a real hard time."

"Don't underestimate them," Dulain warned. "You didn't see any power armor in there and your shuttle got away. I'd be willing to bet the military could take them with minimal casualties. Get them in position regardless. It'll make it easier to strike a different part of the region if you have to."

"I guess I'll turn them loose before we start these interrogations." Christina narrowed her eyes. "Do you think they can be quiet about sending people out of here?"

"Maybe but they'll gnash their teeth about lowering security." Dulain shrugged. "I'll help with that. Give me the coordinates you want them to hit and I'll drop the hint to Reach. You can stay focused and before you say it, don't worry. I'll be sure they do it as quietly as possible. Just find this person you're looking for. What did you call them again?"

"Red Corsair."

"Yeah, them." Dulain turned. "I'll let you get back to it. Keep me informed. Even if I'm not reading the emails, I can still have them at hand for the rare moments of downtime I get."

Christina watched him go, wondering what his job would be like in the future. The intergalactic arena would be different in hundreds of ways. Was Dulain too old school to keep up with it? He was a master of the single planet situation but could he expand himself to include multiple worlds across the universe?

If Christina had to bet, he would be promoted to an admin position. She went through the AIA roster in her head. Part of her worried they might ask her to do it. Of all the operatives, she held the most field experience *and* knew all the big players in the political scene. Her time with Admiral Reach alone made her a prime candidate.

God, I hope they aren't thinking that way. Christina liked working for the AIA, but she had no desire to be the director. After watching Dulain play people for so many years, it stopped appealing to her after about six months. *They always pick the person that doesn't want the job. That's the point.*

Of course, if she failed to reveal Red Corsair, she wouldn't have to worry about a promotion. Christina didn't want to be dramatic but there was a possibility that this person could mean ending much of Earth as they knew it. Even taking down Gamma Alpha in a permanent way would be enough to disrupt defense measures.

The door opened. Essex came in and flopped in the seat beside her. "Alright, I'm ready to start dragging them in. I've got the authorization forms all filled out for their supervisors and we shouldn't run into *too* much trouble." He turned to his tablet. "I even identified the leads with the greatest chance to give us a hard time."

"Good work." Christina sighed. "Dulain visited while you were gone. He's sending the military out there to attack that base. So at least we don't have to worry about that. However, this means we need to be extra diligent as we go about our tasks. Once we get our first ten sequestered, we'll go at them ... then isolate them while we grab the other ten."

"Okay. Sounds like a plan." Essex smiled. "This is so much better than the analyst work I was doing before."

"I thought you'd like going out to the base," Christina replied. "I had no idea you'd this excited about the rest of what we do. Especially what we've been up to for the last few days."

"What can I say?" Essex opened the door for her. "Hanging out with a beautiful lady, looking over files that could mean the end of the world as we know it if we screw up ... what's not to love? Seriously."

"Okay, now you're overdoing it." Christina shook her head. "Let's just go."

***

Cassie rested her head on Vincent's chest, pressing herself against him. After lunch, they slipped away to her quarters, making love for the first time. Part of her regretted their need for haste, the fact they needed to keep track of time but that didn't stop her from reveling in their union, the relief of so much tension.

While he dozed, she listened to his heartbeat, closing her eyes to enjoy the subtle rhythm. *This isn't part of the plan*, Cassie mused to herself as she cuddled against his warmth. *Join the Gnosis, make a name for myself, get a better assignment. That's what I wanted. That's what this was supposed to represent.*

But Vincent worked out. She'd been with men before. Always the guy who was great for that *moment*. She always saw the end of the relationship whether it be on the horizon or around the corner. Career, personality … something always got in the way of keeping things going long term.

Vincent was the first man she couldn't predict an end to their union. Part of that came from the things they experienced together. They'd seen a lot, been through even more. Few people on Earth would ever understand. Aside from their compatibility, they also enjoyed a commonality that felt safe.

That bit was especially fortunate.

Cassie's tablet pinged three times. She thought about ignoring it when she remembered why it had gone off: she had a meeting with her sister in less than ten minutes. "Crap!" She cried, sitting bolt upright. Vincent stirred beside her, resting his hand on her back. "I have to go! Like ... right now!"

"What's wrong?" Vincent asked. "I thought you were done with meetings for the day."

"I forgot about my sister! She's here at Gamma Alpha for some reason." Cassie slipped out of bed, paused ... then turned back to him. Leaning down, she kissed him, gently at first then with more insistence. When it seemed like they might escalate things, she drew back. "Oops! I gotta go! I have to take the world's fastest shower and bolt!"

"How long has it been since you've seen her?"

"A while." Cassie rushed into the bathroom and cranked on the water. "At least a year! We exchange emails sometimes. That's about it. What about your family?"

"They live in Oregon," Vincent called back. "Both parents, my younger sister, two aunts and my grandmother."

"Big family."

"Not particularly. What about you?"

"Tammy and I are the only ones left." Cassie got in the water, wincing at the chill. It warmed as she scrubbed. "Our parents died just before I joined the AIA. We don't really have any extended family. Our grandparents were gone before we were born. I guess anyone more than a sibling seems big to me now."

Vincent stepped into the room. "I get that. How long do you think you'll be?"

"God knows what she wants." Cassie got out of the shower and toweled off. "If it's money, that won't take long. I haven't been able to spend what I make but I doubt she'd come all the way out here for that. Go through the security rigors just to ask me for something? No ... something's going on."

"Well, I hope it's no big deal. Do you want me to come along?"

"Nah." Cassie kissed his cheek as she passed him. "Hang out here. Relax. You're just as busy as I am. I'll come back afterward. Harper and Thayne can't possibly get the Orbs talking before tomorrow. I'm sure we've got some more time. Well ... maybe. When's your leave over?"

"Didn't set a time. Lots of folks are down here. I'll probably be our representative for any small things that come up. Captain will have to come down to deal with planning the attack. Depending on if we're going to be allowed to go along or not. Though I doubt Reach will let us hang back while the Pahxin take care of business."

"Seems unfair." Cassie dressed casually in jeans and a tee shirt. "The Tol'An have plagued the Pahxin for a long time. It should be their problem to deal with. We only recently got dragged into this. But the AIA agrees with Reach. They want us to stick with it to the end, show the Pahxin our will before we have to start negotiating."

"Think it'll be hard?"

Cassie shrugged. "Peacetime changes things. They'll have no reason to be particularly generous at the negotiation table. We've got some decent advocates. We'll just have to see if they'll be enough to make things okay for us." She smiled. "At least they know some of us are smart enough to figure out the Orbs. That'll go a long way."

"And we saved their ambassador," Vincent pointed out. "Don't forget that."

"Yeah, we've got some victories under our belt." Cassie's tablet buzzed again, indicating she was late. "Shit, I have to run. I'll see you soon!" She dashed out the door and ran toward the cafeteria, excusing herself as she bolted past various personnel. A couple had some choice words about running in the hall.

Tammy had always been a bit of a hellion when they were growing up, a challenging girl who pushed their parents hard. After they died, she really went wild and Cassie couldn't do anything to help her. The AIA training program was too intense to take time off to help her through the grief so she got in trouble.

After spending a couple days in jail, she decided to get her act together, really focusing on her studies. She went for physics. The girl was smart, just out of control. Cassie thought she still had time left before she graduated. The educational program she found herself in had been intense enough to keep her constantly busy.

Cassie arrived at the cafeteria a good five minutes late to their scheduled time. Tammy sat in the back. They shared the same dark brown hair and blue eyes but that's where the similarities stopped. Where Cassie was lean from years of physical work in the AIA, Tammy was softer around the edges, not quite pudgy but definitely on the plus size.

Hurrying over, Cassie sat down with a quick sigh. "Sorry I'm late." She looked her sister over, noting she'd dressed up for the occasion in a gray skirt suit. She felt terribly underdressed suddenly. "It's pretty crazy around here so I've been really busy. What's going on? Is everything okay?"

"Hi," Tammy said. "We could start with that."

Cassie smiled. "Sorry. Hi. I've been to so many meetings, we rarely even begin with greetings. But you came a long way and went through a lot to see me. I doubt you're here for pleasantries."

"I thought I should tell you in person," Tammy replied. "I'm selling the house."

Cassie sat up straighter. "Why? I thought we talked about it. One of us was going to live in it someday."

"It's not going to be you." Tammy shrugged. "And I don't want to live in that town. We can split the money but I've already got a buyer."

"Wow. You didn't even talk to me before you started the process?"

"I needed to make some things happen and you weren't even on the *planet*, Cas." Tammy shook her head. "You don't answer my emails, you don't contact me. What should I have done?"

"Waited," Cassie replied. "Until you could talk to me."

"Well, I didn't." Tammy shrugged.

"Is that why you came here?"

"Partially." Tammy looked down at the table, fiddling with a ring on her finger. "I'm ... engaged."

"Wait, what? You're getting married?"

Tammy nodded.

"Don't you have some more school?"

"I do ... but I'm almost done with my graduate program then I'm hitting the books right away for my doctorate." Tammy met her eyes. "He's a good guy. Another physicist. We met in a study group and hit it off."

"Congratulations ... I mean, I'm still kind of pissed about the house but at least that's good news. I don't want half the money. I just wanted to know I could go home again someday. It's going to be weird not having it around."

"You can never go home again," Tammy said. "I promise you it's true. I tried. I went there and spent a weekend. The place was full of ghosts. Mom and dad ... us ... I don't know. I didn't feel comfortable, not for ten minutes. When I left, I vowed never to go back. Even the town feels weird."

"That sucks." Cassie looked away. "Still, I would've liked to try myself. Are you sure you can't stop the sale?"

"I need the money anyway." Tammy scowled. "We can't hold on to things strictly for sentimentality. That doesn't even make sense. We have to move on. That's what you did when you got this job. I'm doing the same thing."

"That sounds pretty final." Cassie leaned forward. She reached for her sister's hand but Tammy recoiled. "What is it you're telling me?"

"When I sell the house and you get your cut of the money, we're done."

"Done?" Cassie lifted her brows. "What does that even mean? Why would you say that? What the hell did I do to you?"

"You remind me of mom." Tammy glared at her. "And honestly, I can't handle it. Besides, you've done everything you can to make yourself a stranger anyway. It's not a hardship for me to walk away from this. I'm ready to start a new life and that means letting go of the old one."

"It was that bad, huh?" Cassie clenched her fist to avoid yelling. "That traumatizing? How long have you been thinking about this? Since you went and spent a shitty weekend at our house? Or was it when you knew I'd be pissed off that you're selling the house from under me? Let me tell you, Tammy your timing could *not* be worse."

"When would be better?"

"Literally, any other time." Cassie rested her head in her hand, closing her eyes. "You have no idea what I've been through. What I've seen or done."

"And I'm sure you can't even tell me."

•

"Actually, I could." Cassie looked her in the eyes. "I could tell you all kinds of things but you're here to cut me out of your life. To end our relationship for ... God knows why. This ... get on with your life thing is kind of bullshit. I'm not sure why you think I deserve that but if this is the decision you've come to, I'm not going to fight it. I'm busy."

"Then ... I guess ... this is over."

Cassie shrugged. "I guess so." She stood. "You might want to see about getting out of here as soon as possible though you'll probably be in line. You didn't have to come here in person to tell me off. It would've been just as kind by email. Or not at all. If the money would've turned up in my account, it would've been just as cold blooded."

"They'll need your signature." Tammy looked away, finally showing some sign of shame.

"Ah. Of course. Now you need me." Cassie shook her head. "Email. I don't want to do ... whatever this was ... again. Later." She left the room. Anger made it hard to think. Part of her wondered why she didn't cry but she'd been through too much to give in to something like that. No, she figured she'd have a drink, relax with Vincent and fight through it.

One way or another, Tammy wasn't going to ruin her time off. Even if she had to get drunk to drown out the nonsense she'd just been subjected to. Her family life already barely existed. Witnessing it die felt like an appropriate companion to the end of the Tol'An. Everything had to end sometime. She just didn't think she'd lose her sister so soon.

***

Ezria sat in his chambers, looking over holographic star map of the galaxy. He had people scouring the galaxy for Gizan, looking to capture or kill him as they could. So far, many had disappeared. His people suggested they might've died or been captured by the authorities. Either situation disturbed him.

They were supposed to be solid soldiers, they type that Gizan himself would've been proud of. If the man was dispatching multiple followers at a time, then he was a bigger problem than Ezria anticipated. It would make sense given the fact he was a formidable killer, the type of man who never failed until he did.

I wonder if I may have been too hasty to punish him. Ezria entertained the thought a few times. *If I hadn't, then what would the others have thought? That favorites were allowed? No, locking him up was the right thing to do even if he didn't think so. He gave me no choice ... then immediately failed me again on his second chance.*

The fact that his best man made two mistakes gave him some pause. Were the humans so dangerous? Or was it the fact that the Pahxin were finally leveraging real military assets to fight them? He didn't know but either way, it frustrated him to no end. That led to a thought, one which felt like he should've had much sooner.

I know where Earth is. Ezria tapped the console to bring the planet upon the star chart. *If I assemble the fleet, if I send them now, then we can finish this once and for all.* His spies confirmed the Trindisha's never made it back to Pahxin space. They must've been kept on Earth. Likely as a means of throwing off the scent of their location.

They had managed to steal the others right out from under rightful Tol'An holdings. That was about to end. When they collected them all, when all six were in their possession, Ezria would finally see true ascension. His organization would rule the galaxy, bringing the order Calatha long saw for them.

But he needed to acquire them and that meant sending in a powerful force, one with enough strength to crush the opposition or at least hit their pathetic base swiftly enough to leave with the Trindishas. That meant calling upon his agent, the traitor who already failed once. It was not ideal, but the man needed to prove himself.

Ezria wanted to punish him for his earlier failure but the Gizan situation had taught him something. The man had to be sweating if the Tol'An agent gave him any indication of the price for failure. It would make him more effective in getting his militia to step in when his people arrived. Their combined efforts would easily take the human base.

He put out the word for his men to assemble and prepare for the attack. It would take several hours to arrive. The surprise attack would be swift and merciless and pave the wave for a universe of peace ... under his careful guidance. Such was the fate of the stars and society as a whole.

***

Desmond was awoken by an urgent message from the surface, Admiral Reach pinging his personal line. He rolled out of bed, tapping the console to bring it online. Leaning forward, he squinted into the camera, blinking several times as he tried to chase away the sleep fogging up his brain.

"Bradford," he muttered. "Hello?"

"Good morning," Reach said. "Glad to see you got some rest. Harper says we're ready to try this thing out. I want you there. Can you be down in two hours?"

Desmond considered the timing. If he contacted the hangar right away, it was possible, providing he got priority clearance. Which didn't seem to be a problem considering who was making the request. He rubbed his eyes and nodded. "I'll throw myself together and be down as soon as possible."

"Sounds great." Reach smiled. "This is it, Desmond! I can feel it! I'll have a war council standing by. Your friends from the Stalwart will be there too! What're you waiting for, man? Get your ass moving! Reach out!"

Desmond rubbed his face, taking a moment to recover from the unbridled enthusiasm of his boss. He'd never seen the man so ecstatic before. They'd fought together, seen wars come and go but he'd never been quite so exuberant. Of course, this was more than just finishing up a border dispute or settling unrest in a small region.

This was all of outer space. A conflict that began on the eve of humanity's first foray into the frontiers of their own solar system. They entered a war they didn't want, a conflict none of them imagined and they were about to come out on top. With the kind help of some new allies and a whole lot of luck.

Desmond let the hangar know to prep a shuttle for immediate launch. He then went about cleaning up and packing a few things for the trip. He figured he'd be on the surface for at least a couple of days. The final step involved leaving Zach Caplan in command of the ship. Everything else was in order and the current tasks were all underway.

The shuttle ride happened faster than he anticipated. Reach gave clearance the moment he had them prep for launch. Engines idled when he boarded and within five minutes, they were on their way to the surface, barreling down at the maximum safe velocity. He didn't notice so much in orbit but when they hit atmo, he grabbed the safety bar.

I hope Reach isn't working himself up for nothing. Desmond worried it might take Harper and her crew longer to establish a connection to the desired devices. If that was the case, then there'd be a lot of important people standing around for nothing. Who else did the man invite? The guys above the admiral tended to be impatient men.

Desmond glanced at his tablet. A priority coded message popped up, letting him know that marines were dispatched to attack a potential terrorist threat in the mountains. That didn't surprise him. The AIA had been working on finding the people responsible for the Gamma Alpha attack. If they found a target, however unlikely, the military would want a crack at them.

They didn't send him troop number but let him know that people from Gamma Alpha and several military bases were conducting a joint action to attack the enemy fortification. Admiral Reach and Dulain were behind the choice to send them out, another part that didn't surprise Desmond. They'd been working together quite a bit.

After the Admiral got over the fact he'd been spied on for the better part of two years by his aide. Desmond often wondered if Cassie was sent to report on him if her sole purpose on the ship was really to keep tabs on the Gnosis. If so, they picked a new tactic by hiding their agent in plain sight.

I can't believe it, Desmond thought. *Cassie's been straightforward every time she needs to be. I'm sure she reports on our actions but there's nothing special to talk about that doesn't end up in official reports. Unless she's trying to judge us based on our competency, I have to believe she's on the level.*

The shuttle touched down and though Desmond had distracted himself throughout the trip, he still felt grateful it ended safely. Disembarking, he found Admiral Reach waiting for him nearby. The man waved, rushing forward to shake his hand. Idling engines made conversation impossible so they hurried off toward the main entrance.

"Sir," Desmond waited until they were inside to speak. "I hope you've tempered your expectations. I hope we're going to be the only ones there in case it doesn't work."

"Yes, I'll have only a few senior Gamma Alpha staff. I started to worry they might explode early this morning."

That thought hadn't occurred to Desmond.

"Are you sure it's wise for you to be there?"

Reach waved his hand dismissively. "I'm not going to miss this moment. I'm confident in Harper, Thayne, and Gil. Not to mention the dozens of others who have been working on this technology since we first discovered it. We're in good hands, Desmond. I only hope they have some idea of how to get them all talking."

They arrived at the lab and stopped outside the door. "If you need anything, they've got a small kitchenette area inside now. Many of them have worked nonstop since you brought back the fourth Orb. They have water, tea, coffee ... that kind of thing. Otherwise, I thought we might just camp out and answer messages while we waited."

"Sounds good," Desmond replied as they stepped into the room. The moment the door opened, they were greeted to the sound of shouts from different technicians. Since they kept talking over one another, it was impossible to make out what they were trying to say and Harper didn't seem to be doing anything to calm them down.

This isn't going to be conducive to answering messages. Desmond looked around, catching sight of Cassie nearby. She was observing but seemed to be staying out of the way of the people rushing around the area. He excused himself from Reach and approached, tapping her on the shoulder.

"Hi Captain," Cassie said. She seemed subdued. "Welcome to a new type of chaos."

"Looks like it." Desmond made a show of looking around. The four Orbs were set in a semi-circle with two spots left open. That intrigued him. He didn't think they would be so optimistic as to believe they would have the opportunity to bring them back there. "How're things going? How long have you been here?"

"Just a few minutes," Cassie said. "Harper called to let me know things were good. I hopped down as soon as I could."

"Reach woke me up. What do you think will happen?"

Cassie shrugged. "The first step was to establish a link between the different Orbs. We've done that already. Now, they're going to use the power of all four to reach out to the others. I've got a few ideas of how to make that work. Unfortunately, our interface device isn't working yet or anyone could do it."

"Meaning we have to rely on you, Gil or Heat to pull this off?"

"Heat hasn't really practiced this at all," Cassie said. "So he probably wouldn't be a good choice. Gil and I understand the basic concepts. He kind of ... got sucked into it." She turned to him. "Not that I'm looking forward to it, mind you. Connecting up to this thing scares the hell out of me every single time."

"I can't even imagine what it's like." Desmond examined her face, noting she wore a carefully neutral expression. "I admire the fact you've weathered it so well though."

"I haven't exactly had a choice." Cassie turned to him. "It was either put your mind at risk with an alien technology or let humanity down. Patriotism aside, I've never felt like there's been much of a choice when it comes to this. Just between us, I thought expert on the technology meant my studies. Not active participant in experimentation."

"Do you know why it picked you on that trip back? Why you had the vision?"

"The exact circumstances, no." Cassie shook her head. "But predisposition made it possible. I probably triggered it by a passive thought, something I didn't even realize I'd done. You know, the million little things that pop through your head on a daily basis. One of them put me in touch with the thing ... and set a course."

"Difficult part of that aside, it's pretty incredible."

"Yes. I can admit that much."

Harper shouted for everyone to be quiet. When they all shushed, Desmond had to admit he was impressed. He thought that chaos would've taken a few tries. The doctor had the voice of a drill instructor and all the presence of a field commander. She held her hands up to gather everyone's attention.

"As you know, we've brought these Orbs together to discover the location of the final two." Harper gestured to the four. "They are hooked up and I'm getting solid readings. Gil and Cassie are here to interface with the devices and get us a star map. For the record, we were unable to find the last two because they are actively masking their signatures."

Gil Vaedra stepped forward. He was a Pahxin, an expert on ancient civilizations throughout the galaxy. He'd been with Cassie during their interface attempt. "Two Trindishas were not sufficient to push through the masking. Nor were we able to force them to turn off their obfuscation. Three came closer but we weren't quite there.

"When I tried, I felt some of the security protocols breaking down. With the fourth, we have enough power to push through. Our enemies may have their devices on stealth mode, but we can now override their efforts." Gil gestured for Cassie. "Agent Alexander, would you be so kind as to join me?"

Cassie waved at Desmond, drawing a deep breath before approaching the center of the room. Two chairs had been set up for them. If it proved to be like the last couple of times they tried these things, both would be out of commission throughout the duration of the experiment. He was surprised Vincent hadn't shown up.

Reach stepped up beside him, putting his hand on his shoulder. "Here we go. This is it!"

Desmond shared his excitement but harbored some trepidation of his own. Would interfacing with four Orbs be more trying on the mind? Gil seemed okay after working with three of them. Perhaps there was nothing really to worry about. Now that they'd unlocked the method, how bad could it possibly be?

It's alien technology, Desmond thought. *God only knows how bad it could get … and what long term effects it has on Cassie, Gil or any of us standing in proximity. In our hour of need, no one stops to think about the risks so much as the rewards. I hope we can get over that soon. It would be nice to worry about safety first.*

Chapter 3

Gizan sat staring into space as he waited for them to emerge from hyperspace. He figured it would take several hours. It was plenty of time for him to make peace with his decision, to prepare himself for what would likely be his death. The odds were stacked cleanly against him.

There are many soldiers there but when I arrive, I have only to kill one man to finish this whole situation. One individual will end this organization once and for all. Success means real freedom. Failure means death. Either is preferable to running for the rest of my life like some sort of frightened animal.

Rythi proved to be far more amenable than Gizan anticipated. The good captain looked forward to a big payday but he was also something of a Pahxin patriot, at least he acted like it when they discussed the coordinates. They'd be arriving on the fringe of the system, allowing them an opportunity to scope the opposition before sliding into the planet.

Gizan anticipated a great deal of trouble but Rythi made it clear he'd landed on many planets without permission. He claimed to have never been caught doing such infiltrations. The man didn't say it with any arrogance either. It seemed entirely possible. *Perhaps I inadvertently picked the perfect partner.*

Rythi fought in several wars before leaving the Pahxin behind. He got into some trouble, primarily for illegal trade. Nothing too bad. If he was able to bank on what Gizan had him doing, he could probably get back in the good graces of his fellows. Of course, that was if Ezria died and the Tol'An folded.

I believe it will happen but I cannot be absolutely certain. This is a mission of chance and recklessness, opportunity and danger.

"We'll be out in a moment," Rythi called out. "When we arrive, I'll need to find some space rocks, anything we can hide out in. I'll run cool until then. From there, we can use the interference from those objects to mask our scan signature. They *might* know someone's looking but they'll have no idea from where."

"You've done this before?" Gizan asked.

"Yes, back in the military we did this kind of thing all the time. I acted as a scout, checking out enemy installations before sending in attack forces. It was dangerous but I learned a lot about not being seen. That's kind of the point, after all." Rythi chuckled. "Of course, my first few attempts weren't entirely successful."

"I suspect you've had to get into some brawls then."

"Back then, yeah. Lately, not so much. To be honest, you're frighteningly good. I normally have much better hearing than that. I haven't had someone sneak up on me in years. Kudos."

"That's what I'm good at." Gizan joined him in the cockpit. "We never discussed the exact terms of our arrangement. I know it's difficult to make promises given that I'm not sure what we'll find, but I can ensure you get all the supplies your ship can carry. There are weapons you might sell … rations. That sort of thing."

"I'm good with that," Rythi said. "I've got a Kalrawv buyer who picks up my guns whenever I happen on them. He's a good guy. Not entirely honest but who can be these days, huh?"

"I suppose that's a point," Gizan replied. He let out a sigh. "Do you ever long to be in a single place?"

"Nah, I couldn't imagine it. That's why I took to the fringe. I thought I might be playing it a bit too dangerous with the authorities. I can't imagine prison. To me, that's the worst thing that could happen to anyone, you know?" Rythi clicked his tongue. "No, for me, I've got to be free to roam the stars. That's my destiny."

"I'm glad to hear for your sake you have achieved it." Gizan leaned against the wall. The ship trembled slightly as they left hyperspace. *Welcome home*, he thought. *How I thought I'd never see this place again.*

"Okay, quick burst scan ..." Rythi muttered. "Yep! I knew it. Always! There's some space junk only ten-thousand kilometers away." He flipped several switches. Lights turned out behind them and it started to get cold. "Once we get there, I can engage the systems again but for now ... well ... it gets chilly."

"I'm noticing." Gizan frowned, peering outside. They were in open space, the planets of the system little more than pinpricks. "How long do you think it'll take to get to the planet from here anyway?"

"Twelve hours at max speed," Rythi said. "I'll use some tricks to make that quicker. When we get close to the natural satellite, we'll make our move and land. I can get you pretty close to the installation too. I've got a little diversion tech onboard. Rarely use it ... but it's designed for just this kind of action."

"I see. Will we be able to listen to their communications?"

"Sure will. Even from out here." Rythi got them moving with a couple quick thruster bursts. "Okay, we'll be there in fifteen minutes." He stood. "Be right back. I need to get the systems online back there. They're manual so they don't draw from the main power ... just in case we have to run *really* cool."

"This is fascinating," Gizan said. "I never knew that a single man could run a ship so effectively."

"You learn to," Rythi yelled back. "What about you? Have you ever thought about settling down? Getting away from this life?"

"I have," Gizan replied. "And upon doing so, I find myself in this situation."

"Ah. The past won't let go."

"Indeed, it will not."

"Sometimes, you have to smack the hell out of it to get your way." Rythi chuckled again. "Though I don't have to tell you that. You've probably seen it plenty of times."

"Not as many as you'd think." Gizan squinted out the window. "We seem to be rapidly approaching your rocks."

"Nah, we've got at least another five thousand kilometers. They just look big, believe me."

Regardless of the captain's reassurance, Gizan didn't feel confident. He began to get nervous when Rythi remained in the back for almost another minute. When he returned, he took his time sitting down, peering casually at the scanner. It took considerable will not to protest the man's relaxed demeanor.

"And ... a little retro rocket," Rythi said, engaging the reverse thrusters. The ship began to slow. "There we are! Drifting right along with them like garbage. Oh, but for the number of times I've ended up having to play *that* role." He sighed. "Okay, time to hit the scans and get you something to listen to."

Gizan rubbed his forehead, surprised at how much sweat built up despite the cool air. Heat kicked in a few moments later. A projection of their destination appeared on the cockpit window, showing a large fleet formation. They were clustered near one of the space stations with others falling in beside them.

"Wow," Rythi said. "That's a lot of ships." He hit a button. "Let's hear what's going on."

"Report in," a voice said. "We are departing in less than five hours. I need sound off from all vessels."

"No ..." Gizan smiled. "They are going off to perform some mission or other. This ... could not be more perfect."

"You're right about that," Rythi said. "We should have no problem landing there now!"

"Excellent." Gizan patted the man on the shoulder. "Pipe this to the back and plot your course. We should figure out how we can close in so we're in the perfect position when they're ready to depart. Good work, Captain. You're proving to be a far better bet than I ever would've anticipated."

"Glad to be of service," Rythi replied. "Sending the com feedback now.

***

Cassie made eye contact with Gil, smiling as she approached. She sat first and he patted her shoulder, a simple gesture she desperately appreciated. The fact they had been through this more than once didn't make it any easier for her to stomach. There was still fear, still a sense that she might not make it out of there with her mind intact.

Harper moved between the two of them, carrying a wire from the main console. She plugged it into a box behind them. Cassie winced as the doctor applied cool gel to her temples before pressing two electrodes against her. They stuck tight, feeling tight and uncomfortable in their position.

"Alright," Harper said. "We've learned a great deal since we started trying to build the item that would allow us to interface with the Orbs directly. While we do not have the device, the one we do have will give you two ready access to information without the esoteric hope that you have a psychic connection.

"It essentially sends the same impulses into your brain as we registered during the experiment. You'll likely go unconscious for the duration. We're going to give you exactly fifteen minutes to find what we need. At that time, we'll pull the plug and hopefully, you'll have what we need.

"If for some reason you need more time, we'll take a short break before we try again." Harper patted Cassie on the shoulder. "Does anyone have a concern?"

Cassie wanted to raise her hand but she remained still. She couldn't see anyone but the silence was telling. Only the occasional cough made it clear she wasn't completely alone. Tension filled the room thick enough to stifle her and she had to take several deep breaths to remain calm.

"Thank you, everyone," Harper said. "Here we go. Brace yourselves, Gil ... Cassie. This *might* sting a little but ... I can't be a hundred percent sure about that. Just try to remain calm and don't move too much. Everything'll be fine."

Easy for you to say, Cassie thought. *You're just sitting over—*

A jolt of pain tore through Cassie's body, making her go rigid. She arched her back, her jaw dropping in a silent scream. The pain vanished almost just as fast but she dared not open her eyes. No sound reached her, nothing but the gentle thrum of power surging through the room. It made her hair stand on end.

She swayed and a strong hand gripped her by the elbow. Cassie turned to see Gil holding her up. They were standing in the center of the room though totally alone. Only the Orbs remained, each one throbbing with white light. She peered around the room, noting it had some small differences.

Like the lack of a door.

"What happened?" Cassie asked. "Why's it look like this?"

Gil hummed. "It's a familiar space for us. The door's missing, yes, but otherwise, it looks the same. Better than the white room we visited before, don't you think?"

"No argument there." Cassie stepped forward. "But what're we supposed to do? When we were in the white room, we just talked to it and things happened. You think it's the same way here?"

"I think we can access the information from the console this time." Gil gestured to the terminal they traditionally used to perform data queries. "Which is a bit more comfortably familiar for us I believe. Although, it's just a proxy for what we're actually doing ... an easier way to understand the motions."

"Yeah, I get it. You want a crack at it? And was that painful to you?"

"Excruciating." Gil shook his head as he walked over to the panel. "I'll be having a word with Doctor Harper about her definition of what is painful." He tapped the terminal screen. "Okay, let's see if we can crack the security. You want to take the secondary station? I think we can work in tandem."

Cassie approached her screen. It flickered to life, displaying an unfamiliar interface with a circle on the left and right and two at the top. A blank space between them glowed white. She tapped the circle on the left and it shimmered, displaying English text in the middle. It read *indicate the function you wish to utilize*.

"Are you getting this too?" Cassie asked.

"Yes," Gil replied. "Seems that we can use one at a time or all together. If you tap each of them in turn, they'll all glow. Then we can patch into security."

Cassie smiled. "You make it sound like you've done this before."

"More like thought about it a lot." Gil turned to her. "But this is different than expected. It is interesting that the interface looks the same for both of us. That either means I'm becoming more in touch with humans or you're leaning toward the Pahxin." He nudged her with his elbow. "I'm not sure which I prefer."

Cassie laughed. "Nice thought but you've been hanging around more humans than I have Pahxin."

"But think about all the contact you've had with alien civilizations. Those were our predecessors. Anyway ... I think I'm ready." Gil leaned to look at my screen. "Tap those globes so they're all shimmering."

Cassie complied. The text in the center changed, stating *security function override in process.* "That looks like a good thing, huh?"

"Maybe we'll have something go our way for once." Gil shrugged. "It could happen."

A red light flashed on the screen, several quick strobes. "You jinxed us, Gil." Cassie tapped the screen and the word *warning* appeared. *Devices are in shadow mode. Please confirm authorization to attach to these devices.* "Um ... I don't see anything indicating that allows me to do that."

"How about we just say it like before?" Gil cleared his throat. "I confirm authorization. Please connect to the devices." Nothing happened. When Cassie looked at him, he shrugged. "It was worth a try."

Cassie tapped the screen. It changed to one of her standard query apps, the ones she'd used to gather information from the Orb many times in the past. She typed at the keyboard, performing her typical login. The system paused, just as it always had in the past before popping up with a message showing her credentials were accepted.

"This is so weird." Cassie went into the settings. A large red button appeared with the word *authorize* on it. She tapped it.

Secondary authorization required. Cassie turned to Gil. "Probably because we're both here. You want to get on that terminal?"

"I'm not sure what it's going to bring up." Gil returned to his terminal, typing away. "Ah … it's one of our old standards from my education days. Fascinating where it draws these from. It must delve into the deepest recesses of our minds for the thing we're most comfortable with to use."

"Too bad it didn't do that when we did the experiment," Cassie pointed out. "Hurry up. We're short on time here." A timer displayed on her terminal showing they had less than five minutes. "How the hell did we chew through ten minutes so fast? I swear to God we've been standing here for less than five."

"We probably weren't conscious for the first several." Gil tapped quickly. "Alright, I'm authorizing now."

Cassie's screen changed, showing the four Orbs again. Two more appeared, this time on the bottom. They began to blink, slowly at first then with increasing speed. The words *establishing connection* appeared. "Do you think it's going to give us a location or just allow us to access them?"

"Likely both," Gil said, "but I am just guessing. However, interesting to note. What if we could blow one of them up?"

"You can't be serious," Cassie replied. "I can't believe you even offered that option."

Gil shrugged. "It would save the military a lot of time."

"You of all people shouldn't even be thinking about destroying a culturally significant item like that." Cassie shook her head. "No, we don't have any idea what would happen. These could be anywhere, including some populated area. We have no idea what their base looks like. It would be irresponsible to just destroy them arbitrarily."

"I think the Pahxin would agree with the possibility of losses," Gil replied. "They might consider it an equitable trade."

"Even if the leader isn't there?" Cassie asked. "I know you're good with this whole archaeology thing but think about the military implications of destroying something without visual confirmation of the target. We could just prolong the conflict *and* destroy something without cause. No. We can't do it. I won't agree to it."

"Alright." Gil turned back to his screen. "It was just a thought we needed to entertain. After all, we've been looking for the Tol'An for a *very* long time. My government might be willing to do just about anything to eliminate them once and for all. Even destroying a planet." He smirked. "But … this is coming from a man who was practically an outlaw when we met."

"Yeah, remember that." Cassie gave him a sidelong glance. "You can't speak for them. Your perspective on their behavior is seriously skewed. Just … you know. Relax. We'll let the military decide. If for some reason they bring up destroying one of the Orbs, I'll push back but at least it'll be a military idea instead of us making things up from in here."

The lights stopped flashing and all the circles on her screen went solid white. A line traced between them. The connection established and the devices in the room lit up so brightly Cassie had to shield her eyes. Gil shouted in surprise then told her to look at something. She squinted but didn't see anything.

Then it became obvious. A star chart floated above the chairs they'd been sitting in before. As the lights around them died down, a single line appeared on the map. One started at Earth and the other terminated some distance off. Cassie had no idea where that might be or how far away it was.

"That sector …" Gil shook his head. "That's what you would call the middle of nowhere. I wonder if we've even charted it." He sighed. "We're going to have to do some research with an up to date star database. Hopefully, one of the Pahxin vessels orbiting the planet will have what we need."

"That far, huh?" Cassie tried to calculate the distance but it was difficult to tell with the chart. "How long would it take to get there?"

"Depends on our calculations," Gil said. "But it's far so they'll be complicated. I would say minimally … eight hours. Possibly fifteen. Modern technology might make a fool of me though. Hyperspace drives have come a long way since I messed with them. I'm sure Thayne will give us an accurate estimate when we get out of here."

"So you have the coordinates?" Cassie asked.

"I do." Gil pointed at her screen. "They're going to wake us up in less than forty seconds."

"Timing." Cassie chuckled. "They probably needed to give us twenty minutes."

"Lucky it only took fifteen ... this interface though. It's so strange that this is what the Orbs chose. I wonder what it will be like when we have the device to talk to it." Gil looked at the Orbs nearby. "The mysteries we continue to unlock has been nothing short of shocking to me. I sincerely cannot get over all that we have yet to learn."

"Crap!" Cassie slapped her thigh. "Do you think they know we just found them?"

Before Gil could answer, Cassie gasped, sitting forward on her chair. A dozen people surrounded her, each hovering entirely too close. Questions started bombarding her, so many voices she couldn't differentiate them. She held up her hand to stave them off, to get a second to breathe but they wouldn't let up.

"Stop!" Cassie muttered. "Hold on!" She rubbed her eyes with the heels of her hands, grinding them in for several moments to fend off a low ache. Someone touched her arm and she shook away. "Give me some space! Please!" But they still didn't back off. Someone became more insistent, shouting.

When she opened her eyes again, the room appeared to be silent. No one crowded her but Harper stood nearby. Cassie cleared her throat and stood. "Um ... hello?" She touched the back of her neck when a sharp pain danced down her spine. "Ouch ... that was ... really strange. And entirely more intense than I anticipated."

"Are you okay?" Harper asked. "You kind of freaked out when we woke you up just now."

"Must've been ..." Cassie shrugged. "I don't know. Some kind of post-traumatic stress from interfacing with the Orb I guess."

"Did you get the information?" Reach called out. "Whatever happened, did you at least manage that?"

Cassie nodded. "Yes, we have the coordinates for the other two Orbs." She looked around. The other chair was empty. "Where's Gil? He ... said he memorized it."

"Ah." Harper cleared her throat. "He didn't wake up right away. We moved him to the medical bay. Do you remember the information?"

"I can bring it up on a star chart." Cassie approached one of the terminals, half expecting it to show the circles again. It remained normal. She brought up a navigation screen and drew the same line she saw before. "There it is. That's what we saw. We were able to override the security feature and locate both of them."

"Yes!" Reach clapped his hands together. "We started to get worried after a couple hours but you came through! Great work, Agent Alexander. Fantastic!"

"Wait, what?" Cassie raised her brows. "What do you mean a couple hours? You were going to wake us up in fifteen minutes."

"Cassie ..." Harper put her hand on her shoulder. "We did. You guys went back in several times. You don't remember?"

"I ..." Cassie shook free. "I can't believe this. Are you serious? Is that ... so wait, Gil and I have been under over and over?"

"You both insisted," Harper replied. "Gil didn't wake up about half an hour ago but you said you were good to go."

"This is crazy!" Cassie backed away, bumping into the chair. "There's no way! It was only fifteen minutes! There was a timer and everything! Hell, I was *talking* to Gil just before I woke up right now! We were debating ... something important." She pinched the bridge of her nose. "Something about ... no ... it was ... security I think."

"We should get you to the medical bay," Harper said. "They need to look you over."

"No ... I'm fine ... I think. I'm good." Cassie shook her head. Was she actually standing amongst those people? Were they real? She didn't know but part of her doubted. After all, they'd all been yelling a few moments before and then they were silent. Was this another hallucination? "How do I know I'm really awake?"

"Oh boy." Harper turned away. Two technicians came forward.

"What are you doing?" Cassie looked between them. "Back off. I'm serious. I woke up and there was shouting then ... nothing. And now you're telling me I've been going back in there over and over? This has to be a trick. This isn't normal. Where's Vincent? He would be here if this was real."

"I'll get him," Desmond spoke up. So at least the captain was present. That gave Cassie *some* hope. "Hang tight!"

"Why isn't he here now?" Cassie shuffled back from the technicians. "Where is he?"

"Only authorized personnel were in the room," Thayne spoke up this time. He came forward, his hand outstretched, palm up. "Please, Cassandra. I'll take you to the sick bay myself. We'll get Vincent to meet us on the way. You just need a moment to acclimate to being back up and about."

"But how do I know this isn't part of my mind playing tricks?"

"If it is," Desmond said, "what will it hurt going to the medical bay?"

"No. I ... I want my tablet." Cassie looked around. "Where is it? I'll contact Vincent myself."

Desmond stepped forward. "Here you go." He extended her tablet. "I'll walk with you out of the room. You know you can trust me." He stared into her eyes. "Right?"

Cassie looked at the others around her. Of all the people in the room, he did count as the one least likely to be playing games with her. If the situation happened to all be in her head, then he'd be a safe bet. After all, she'd imagine him the same way he was in real life: a decent, forthright person.

Not that she had much of a choice. If she didn't trust someone soon, they'd probably lock her up. And if she happened to be in the real world, then God only knew how long they'd keep her that way. Better to err on the side of caution. At least then she'd be able to see what happened to Gil.

"Okay," Cassie replied, taking the tablet from Desmond. "I'll go with the captain." As they left, a pall of tension seemed to lift. She didn't think she made that part up but it was hard to say for sure. *God, I hope this comes out okay. I really don't want to be in a padded cell during the final mission.*

***

Captain Jeffrey Kent sat near the hatch of their dropship, clinging to his rifle. High command picked him to lead the mission on the mountain base. They had a decent amount of information to go on, a fair layout of the area but the one thing they lacked was troop density. Specific numbers were not available.

Best guess from intel was less than two hundred with conventional weapons. They wouldn't have any armor to speak of but they could be dug in deep. Their dropship would provide air support while they swept the base clean. They were to kill or capture all combat personnel in the area.

The basic sweep shouldn't have been too terrible, especially with sixty armored marines and fifty conventional backup troops standing by. What bothered Kent was the unknown factor. If these people were working with traitors, then they might have access to advanced technology, something they planned to use for another attack on Gamma Alpha.

When he brought up his concern, he was told that was why they were being sent to attack the facility. Better they fight on the enemy's home territory than their own. That seemed like common sense but it still didn't make him feel any better about finding out they had ray guns, or at least something capable of bringing down their air support.

Lieutenant Brady Dashwood sat beside him. They'd run countless missions together, mostly in Africa and Asia. When the power armor became available, the two of them were second in line to train with it. The others went with the Gnosis while the rest remained at Gamma Alpha, continuing to practice while essentially being on guard duty.

Dashwood established a private connection to Kent. "These are the same guys we fought back at the base, right?"

"Apparently. I hope it's all of them. I don't want to spend the next six months chasing them all over the globe."

"If they're working with traitors," Dashwood pointed out, "it could take to the stars, right?"

"Nah, I've heard a rumor that we're about to take down the bastards that started this shit. The Tol'An? I think that's what they're called. Apparently, those aliens we've been working with are planning to send a badass fleet out there to tear them up. Providing we find out where they're hiding out."

"Think the Gnosis will go?"

"Probably. We have to be represented."

"You sad we're not going?"

Kent shrugged. "I don't really care. I'm here to do my job wherever they need me. They want me to go out there and kill aliens on some other planet? Just gotta ask. Otherwise, we seem to find plenty of people on Earth to blast. Case and point, look what we're doing right now."

"Red was telling me there could be aliens at the base," Dashwood said. "They might be there to support these bastards."

"I don't know where he gets his info but," Kent held up his hand, "I am worried about weapons. They might have something more advanced than a couple automatic rifles and grenades. If that's the case, this armor might not be the *I win* card we're hoping for. But intel doesn't have any evidence so ... we go in assuming otherwise."

"I'd rather pretend they've got great gear than be surprised."

"Won't matter either way. We're dropping right on top of the base while our air cover bombards them. Even if they bring out some heavy ordnance, we're going to wreck these guys. You saw how well they did back at Gamma Alpha. Once the element of surprise wore off, we drove them off pretty fast."

The pilot turned on the red light, indicating they were drawing close to their target. "I have visual on the target. We're moving into attack formation. Anti-aircraft weaponry is being discharged. Prepare yourselves for deployment. I repeat, prepare for deployment. All units need to jump in less than three minutes."

Kent stood first, followed by Dashwood. They approached the hatch as the other eight men behind them rose as well. Each ship held ten soldiers, three airships full of armored marines. Their support moved south to a pass wide enough to make an approach viable. They were present only if things went incredibly bad, far worse than anticipated.

I'm not putting those men at risk if I don't have to. Kent made the vow to himself before they even boarded their ships. He complained to the major about even sending them along but the army insisted on having a presence in the field. Somehow, the mission became a prestige op, one that each branch wanted to send a representative for.

How about we worry more about finishing the mission than making people happy? Kent's opinion was shared by his CO but regardless, it didn't matter. High command made their ruling so they had to comply. *If they really wanted to be involved in something big, they should be vying for a spot on the Gnosis when they go take down the space terrorists.*

The ramp dropped and Kent glanced out, ensuring they were genuinely over the target. His altimeter showed they were three hundred feet over the target. He hopped out, engaging his thrusters to control the descent. Other ships opened nearby, more marines spilling out until they dotted the sky, armored titans plunging toward the surface.

Anti-aircraft guns popped all around them, flak filling the air with black smoke. Kent knew it would be a matter of luck whether or not he was hit by the attacks but they weren't aiming at him anyway. The ships were hammering the peripheral defenses, pounding the walls and weapon emplacements.

Kent made out eight standing structures. It was built into the mountain so they would likely have to go inside to finish off their quarry. Intel stated there were other ways for vehicles to depart, a valley nearby with an opening to a small hangar. That would be covered by the third shuttle that veered off as soon as it dropped its men.

The altimeter showed he was less than a hundred feet above the ground. Kent engaged his thrusters, grunting as he rapidly slowed. The ground grew closer and he made out a number of men running around in the open courtyard. Some of them stopped, aiming up to shoot at the descending marines.

Kent returned fire, using his HUD in an effort to get close to his targets. Some of the other marines lobbed missiles down into the base, hammering the area with explosive ordnance. Enemy soldiers were launched into the air here and there, their bodies blasted into pieces from the attacks.

Ten feet above the ground, Kent hit his thrusters again, carrying himself toward a roof. He landed hard enough to make the building shake. He paced to the edge, letting his weapon lead the way. A group of enemies stood below him, firing in the opposite direction at some marines who hadn't made it to the ground yet.

Kent dropped one of his rockets on them, landing it directly in the center of their group. It exploded, tossing body parts in all directions. The conventional weapons proved to be true, at least for the rank and file defenders outside. Several bullets tapped his armor on the left, fired from a weapon that lacked the power to cause any real damage.

He turned and shot back, driving the men away from the window they fired from.

Other marines landed. Chaos reigned around him as his people devastated the enemy ranks. Some of them started running, fleeing back toward the main complex in the center of the base. *That's where they'll have their underground facility— the place they might be able to escape from.*

The shuttle pilots called out that the anti-aircraft emplacements were down. They were moving into an over watch state, leaving the mop up for the marines. The third shuttle already left, moving to find the hangar to catch any evading enemies. With some luck, the whole operation would be over in a few minutes.

But Kent didn't like it. He felt like they marched in far easier than even they anticipated. Something wasn't right but what it might've been, he couldn't say. Hopping off the roof, he joined four other marines as they hustled down a path toward the main building. The occasional bark of rifles greeted them but the sounds were few and far between.

As they approached the doors, they joined six other marines who stood to the sides. "Report," Kent said. "What's going on?"

"They've got some heavier weapons in there," Dashwood replied. "We arrived a moment ago and Albany took a rocket to the chest. We pulled him out for evac but that doesn't seem to be all they've got so we tossed some of our own explosives in. Grenades, rockets … but they're dug in pretty well."

"We have to break in." Kent risked a quick glance inside, snapping a photo with his helmet. He stepped back for cover and admired his shot. It was blurry but that didn't matter. He didn't see any people in the shot. The room was wide open with several metal crates positioned about the area. Scans indicated men stood behind them as cover.

"What the hell are those crates made of?" Kent asked. "Do you see them? They withstood a pretty heavy bombardment if you guys hit them that hard."

"Don't know," Dashwood said. "But they didn't move when we hit them. Might be rooted down somehow? Can't say. But if they're hiding behind them, we're going to have to get creative."

As if to punctuate his point, an energy beam burst through the door, cutting into the wall opposite it. A black mark remained, recessed into the surface though the attack didn't quite go through. While the conventional rifles wouldn't get through the power armor, that thing certainly would. The question was whether it was a handheld device or an emplacement.

If it was the former, that meant some real trouble.

Kent got on the com back to HQ. "Be advised, we have advanced weaponry on the field. Repeat, the enemy has access to energy weapons. We are going to attempt to breach momentarily." He turned to Dashwood. "Now that they know what's going on, we have to find a way through. Thoughts?"

"Blow the building." Dashwood motioned with his head. "No reason to save the structure. We're not occupying this place."

"I like your lack of subtlety." Kent turned to the others. "Everyone get back. I'm calling in a strike." The marines hopped away with jump packs, withdrawing to a safe distance. Dashwood and Kent took position across the wall on the roof with line of sight on the front doors. "Shuttle two, I'm about to paint a target and I need you to hammer it."

"I'm on it. Wheeling around to make the run now."

Kent placed two target marks at the base of the structure. The blasts might not take it down completely but providing it gave another entry point, the job would be done. Another couple energy blasts burst from the door, searing the building they stood on. Something flashed beneath them.

That must've cut through the metal finally, Kent thought. *A couple blasts to get through a metal wall. Even if those are emplacements, they're pretty nasty. I wonder how they got them here.*

The shuttle swept down, blasting the target area in a quick pass. They must've dumped twenty concentrated energy beams before having to pull up and veer off. Several chunks of the wall were gone, massive holes exposing the interior. Part of the roof collapsed. Movement inside indicated at least some of the enemy survived.

"Okay, you got your holes," Kent said. "Time to see what that bought us."

The marines charged, bursting from their various points of cover, laying down suppressive fire into the building through the various new entry points afforded them. A couple of energy blasts fired randomly, one into the air and another too wide to catch anyone. The first of the marines reached the facility and didn't slow down, bursting into the space.

Dashwood followed, keeping just ahead of Kent as they went about securing the space. Kent was about to issue an order when someone shouted "grenade! Take cover!" Fallen bits of debris and the metal crates provided reasonable protection. When the device went off, it shook the foundation of the building.

Kent saw a marine's body thrown clear of the facility, pieces of his armor melted. Someone else screamed twice before going silent. He called for medics, but at least two men were already dead. A passageway led to a flight of stairs going down, shadows dancing on the ceiling as their opponents fled.

"Sound off," Kent shouted. "How many of you are ready to get back in there?"

Even the wounded made it clear they were ready to go on the attack again but Kent couldn't risk everyone. They had a lot of mopping up to do topside. "Dashwood, grab six men. It's too close of quarters for more than eight of us. The rest of you sweep and clear this facility. I want the entire base eradicated in half an hour. You get me?"

His speaker distorted from the shouted *hoo-ah*.

As Kent approached the door, he skirted a scorch mark on the floor. Bits of the metal were cracked, leading away from the point where the grenade went off. Pieces of power armor sat amongst the debris, twisted and broken into chunks. He saw a bone sticking out of one of them but turned away, focusing on the door ahead.

He didn't see any emplacements, no weapons on bipods left behind. He doubted the grenade took them out, meaning they still had to contend with the beam weapons when they went further into the facility. This meant ensuring they had some kind of backup in the event things went south.

"Kent to marine units. When you have finished sweeping the base, converge on this structure again and await orders. If you don't hear from us in twenty minutes, form another team and come looking. It probably means we're screwed. Good luck and we'll see you guys soon."

"That dire, huh?" Dashwood asked. "You think we're in that much trouble?"

"I don't know how many people are down there," Kent replied, "nor do I know what other weapons they have but after that grenade and those beams, I know we're dealing with something we've never seen before. Maybe those men on the Gnosis have, but our targets have all been conventional fighters. Now … we get a chance to try the real thing."

"We're ready." Dashwood nodded to him.

Kent started down the stairs. "Then follow me."

Chapter 4

Christina wrapped up her ninth interview. She felt confident she did not speak to Red Corsair. If they did, they were better actors than she would've given them credit for. She went at them from several angles, trying desperately to trip them up. Only one of them seemed even remotely concerned by the process and he started crying halfway through.

She thought for sure she found someone who was guilty but it turned out he just didn't handle pressure well. Why he'd traveled outside the base as he had didn't make sense but apparently his supervisor pushed him to do it. Christina double checked with his colleagues and proved his story true.

Chances were good the man wasn't cut out for military service of any kind but apparently, he was a brilliant engineer.

So much for that. Christina stepped out to meet up with Essex. *I hope to God he found something*. She leaned against the wall, flipping through messages on her tablet. A message from Dulain caught her attention. The subject was *found it*. She tapped on it, bringing the rest of the mail up on her screen.

Cassie and Gil succeeded. We have the location of the final two Orbs. Unfortunately, Agent Alexander had a rough time. It took longer than expected. She's been escorted to medical. If you have a chance, I'd recommend paying her a visit. It might help. Otherwise, we're going to start a war council soon to determine the best course of action for an attack.

"That's good news," Christina muttered. "At least that part of things is working out."

"Agent Dawson!" Essex shouted. He was running down the hall, shoving people out of the way. She smirked. "Agent Dawson! I found something! I found something!"

"Settle down," Christina said. "You're going to shove a major and end up in the brig. What's going on?"

"When I was interrogating my people, I picked up a signal from outside the system. It was directed at this base!" Essex gestured to his tablet. "It wasn't received by control or any of the standard communication terminals either. Whoever received it was in the dormitory wing. If we hurry, I think we'll find Red Corsair!"

"Lead the way!" Christina gestured. "And hurry!"

They charged through the base, weaving through the hallway until they arrived in the dormitories. Regular personnel took up those quarters. Transients occupied the rooms nearer to the front entrance. These were well appointed apartments suitable for long term residents. Christina hadn't visited the area before.

Essex peered at his tablet gesturing down the hall. "It's over here. Three more doors."

"Whose room is it?"

"I'm not sure," Essex replied. They flanked the door. "Scans show the room is empty but the signal is definitely being broadcast in there."

Christina drew her weapon and kicked the door open, pacing inside to clear the space. A neatly made bed occupied the center of the room opposite a monitor screen. The window across the way had the blinds drawn, a desk positioned directly under it. She pushed open the door to the right, opening to a bathroom and a closet beside that. Both were unoccupied.

"What the hell?" Christina frowned. "Where's the tablet?"

"Drop the weapon," Essex said.

"What?" Christina glanced back at him. He was aiming his pistol at her head. "Are you kidding me? There's no way you're Red Corsair. What are you doing?"

"You were right about the AIA," Essex said. "I don't want to be involved after all, not when I have a better offer on the table."

"Better offer? What the hell are you on about? You're a traitor. Where do you think you can go?"

"There've been some promises but you still haven't dropped that gun." Essex stepped closer to her. "Do it! Now!"

"Just hold on a second—" Essex interrupted her by lashing out, striking her with the butt of his pistol against her shoulder. She winced but didn't go down, didn't so much as move. Glaring into his face, she tossed the weapon on the bed. "You are making a huge mistake. Whatever you think you're going to get out of this, you won't."

"We'll just see about what I get." Essex motioned. "Turn around. I have to make this clean."

"Amazing." Christina lifted her arms, holding them up by her head. "Was there even a signal?"

"Yes, it came through while I was interrogating one of the people and he made me an offer."

"One you couldn't refuse?"

"Won't matter to you." Right when he spoke, Christina spun in place, deflecting his weapon to the side. It went off, putting a hole in the bathroom door. She grabbed his wrist, controlling the gun while using her free hand to clock him in the jaw. He stumbled back, dragging her with him.

Essex bumped into the wall, struggling to free his gun hand. He plowed his knee into her side but she refused to let go. She slammed her forehead into his nose, feeling the bone give under the force. He dropped the gun and shoved her back, throwing a wild punch. The attack caught her on the cheek, spinning her around.

She fell toward the bed where she'd dropped her own gun. Bouncing on the cushion, she snatched the weapon just as Essex grabbed her by the jacket. He hoisted her backward, putting her in a headlock. Christina didn't want to kill him, not right away. He had information she needed but he wasn't giving her much of a choice.

Pressing the gun against his hip, she fired twice. The recoil made the weapon bounce into her, biting into her waist. Each blast made her ears ring, the scent of smoke burned the back of her throat. Something warm coated her side as Essex's grip loosened. He dropped to the ground.

Christina stumbled away, spinning to point the gun at his head before dropping into a crouch. He pressed his hands against his wound, staring up at her in shock.

"You shot me …"

"Shut the hell up." Christina slapped him across the face. "Tell me who got the signal. Right now!"

"I can't …"

Christina shot him in the knee. Her ears hurt far worse with that one but she ignored the pain, ignored his scream. "You don't have time to be crying about a little pain, Essex. Tell me who got the signal. I've got a lot of bullets left before I put one in your God damn face. Now talk!"

"I ... it was ..."

"I know it was one of your ten, you jack ass!" Christina pressed her gun against his other knee. "Answer me!"

"It was Major Albans!" Essex shouted. "We were talking ... and his tablet went off. I looked down at it and the signal came from out of the system, okay? He received some orders!"

"What orders?" Christina pressed the gun harder against his knee. "Talk!"

"Okay! Just settle down! He was ordered to have someone attack Gamma Alpha!"

"When?"

"Now!" Essex closed his eyes tightly. "Apparently, the Tol'An have some kind of plan and they need some help with it, but I don't know more than that! He brought me in, offered me a place with that militia."

"And all you had to do was kill me, huh?" Christina shook her head. "How were you going to explain that?"

"That you were the traitor," Essex replied. "After you were dead, I'd plant some evidence."

"Dulain never would've believed that, you idiot! Jesus Christ, you flushed your life and career for that? I thought you were smart!" Footsteps in the hallway caught her attention, the guards responding to the gunfire no doubt. "I should execute you right here for treason but I'm sure we can get some more out of you."

Guards stepped in, aiming their weapons at her. "Stand down," Christina said. "This man attacked me and betrayed us to the Tol'An. I need you to take him into custody, get him some medical attention and ensure someone's with him at all times. Do you understand? You are *not* to let this man out of your sight."

"Yes, ma'am. Do you need medical attention?"

Christina shook her head as she stood. Plunging her weapon back in its holster, she scowled at Essex. "I'm fine. I need someone to arrest Major Albans right away as well. In fact, while you're dragging this sorry piece of shit to medical, lock the base down. No one gets in or out until further notice."

An alarm went off overhead.

"What the hell is that?" Christina asked.

"I told you they wanted us to attack right away," Essex said. "This is whatever they were planning."

"Fabulous." Christina flipped her com on, sending an urgent request to talk to Dulain. He answered immediately. "I've got so much bad news it's insane. I've got someone heading over to arrest the traitor right now but I think Gamma Alpha's under attack. Do we have any defensive forces here?"

"We do," Dulain said. "And I think you're right though the military hasn't made it obvious yet. Get yourself to me here in Admiral Reach's briefing room. We'll figure out what we can do to help from here. Are you okay?"

Christina touched her cheek where Essex punched her and sighed. She started down the hall at a brisk pace. "Never better, Beaumont. I'll see you in a few minutes."

***

Ulian Hataran arrived for the war council, stepping into the large briefing room in the Gamma Alpha base. He noted several other prominent officials from the Pahxin military along with human commanders as well. Each of them mingled as they waited for the formal meeting to begin.

The potential end of the Tol'An attracted quite the crowd. Most of the people standing around were the types that wanted glory, to claim a spot as a participant in the conclusion to a terrorist threat allowed to flourish for far too long. Ulian felt they misunderstood the true benefit of the action.

Acquiring the last of the Trindishas meant far more than destroying ships and ending the terrorist movement. Yes, they could finally be done with the constant harassment of those bastards but the future of the galaxy would be altered when they brought those devices together.

The fact they were on the verge of doing so should've been the thing people wanted a part of. But the benefits promised to be far more subtle, despite the fact no one knew exactly what would happen. Scholars from the homeworld were en route to be part of the process, to be there when the devices came together.

Ulian spoke with his own technical officers and they refused to speculate as to what sort of wonders they might uncover. The cynical ones amongst his crew suggested nothing new would happen. They thought secrets were gated, only to be discovered when a civilization reached a certain point of maturity.

That was possible though it seemed the devices misjudged several cultures since they died out due to technological advancements. Creativity could turn anything into a weapon, any breakthrough into suicide it seemed. Ulian hoped his own people and the humans learned that lesson well.

Of course, it all depended on who remained in charge of the research after the threat ended. Would the Pahxin demand to have the Trindishas moved back to their own facilities? One theory suggested they were only together one time, back when they were first created. The civilization that built them did so for other cultures.

That meant they should operate ideally when *not* in the same room. It allowed cultures across the galaxy to communicate with one another, create a common language, partner up and function in a way that would've been impossible otherwise. They helped the Pahxin and humans partner in a swift manner.

Captain Desmond Bradford entered the room wearing a worried expression. Ulian wondered what might've happened. As he started over to the man to check on him, a blaring noise sounded overhead. The lights began to flash. He turned his attention to Admiral Reach who scowled, turning to his aide.

"What's going on?" Reach asked. "What's happening?"

Beaumont Dulain, their head of intelligence, spoke up next. "We're under attack."

"More militants?" Reach slapped the table. "I thought the military had them locked down!"

"No, this is happening in orbit." Dulain checked his tablet. "The report suggests Tol'An ships."

Ulian headed for the door. "We need to get to our ships," he said. "Fortunately, there are destroyers up there to keep them busy but flying through that mess will likely be a challenge."

Desmond turned to Reach. "I'll grab Vincent and head up there right away. Most of our marines are down here so they can help defend the base if it comes to that."

"Damn it!" Reach sighed. "I'll organize our defenses here. Fend them off, gentlemen! This could work to our advantage if they've committed too much of their force. We'll crush them here and follow the stragglers back to their base for a coup de grace. Command will open a tactical com net for updates. Good luck."

Ulian rushed out with Desmond close beside. "You looked worried when you entered the room. Did you have a bad feeling?"

"No, one of my crew is in the medical bay," Desmond said. "She's the one who pulled the information we needed to find the Tol'An base."

"Ah, her and Doctor Vaedra. I heard he had a bit of a meltdown."

"So did she. It took a lot longer than anticipated." Desmond shook his head. "We don't have time to worry about it now." He looked at his tablet. "Ten ships ... maybe more have appeared and immediately attacked your outer defensive ships. I hope your destroyers are up to the task until we can jump in the fight."

"It depends on who's come up against us," Ulian said. "And whether we even make it back to our ships without our shuttles being destroyed. But I left my first officer in command and she's ready for her own ship. If for some reason I don't make it back, she'll do fine without me."

"My first officer is here." Desmond gestured. "I have to grab him. We'll talk when we're on our respective bridges, huh?"

"Indeed. Good luck, Captain." Ulian tapped his communicator. "Morala, report. What's going on up there right now?"

"A large Tol'An battle fleet emerged from hyperspace nearby," Morala replied. "We have launched fighters to intercept their attack force. Com channels were jammed up when we tried to reach you. I'm glad you got through. I'm assuming you're on your way up here now? I can provide an escort?"

Ulian paused, listening to an announcement on the speakers overhead. "Ship captains, we have fighters standing by to fly with your shuttles. Please note that all departures are scheduled for the next five minutes. Make your way swiftly to the airfield. This is not a drill. All marines to the walls."

"Sounds like I won't need it," Ulian said. "Get me an accurate count. How many of our ships made it for the war council?"

"There are nine destroyers and two other battleships present," Morala said. "One of them is the *Fortitude*. Do you know Torqua very well?"

Ulian attended the academy with Torqua. They weren't necessarily friends, but each developed a grudging respect for the other. Duty kept them apart for the most part but when they were thrust together, things didn't go well. Neither man approved of the other's methods very well.

Torqua proved to be one of the more headstrong, reckless commanders in the Pahxin fleet. That's why Ulian pushed Morala hard away from that path. He didn't want her to be like his former classmate. Especially when she was so much better at her job, had such keen instincts.

"Yes, I know him." Ulian sighed. "Let me guess, he's taken the Fortitude straight toward the enemy, charging headlong without waiting for backup or even orders, right?"

"That's an affirmative," Morala replied. "I'm curious why he wasn't down there with you."

"Because he likes to make a dramatic entrance." Ulian hummed. "Or he knew something might happen. He's a bit out of control, but he's also clever. It stands to reason we would be attacked though I thought even the Tol'An knew better than to assault such a well-fortified area."

"They could be desperate," Morala pointed out. "After all, we've got four of the Trindishas. Maybe they're worried we can find their base. Better to assault here than dig in and wait back at their home base."

"Good points." Ulian saw the exit up ahead. "I'm almost to the shuttle. Remain at the ready but do *not* engage any of the enemy capital ships until I arrive. See you soon." He killed the connection and picked up the pace, charging across the tarmac to his waiting ship. The pilot was watching the ramp and as he boarded, it immediately closed.

"Welcome aboard, sir. I can get us up and to the ship in less than five minutes, sir." He didn't recognize the man at the controls. He must've been one of the pilots brought in by the Admiralty. "My name's Eyros. We can launch on your command, sir."

"Shouldn't we wait for support?" Ulian asked.

"This ship has scout rated shields and automated turrets," Eyros replied. "The Tol'An have yet to get their fighters in position as well. I'm certain we can make it without needing escorts. The Stalwart is also close by in a low orbit."

"Alright then, I'll trust your judgment." Ulian strapped himself in. "Get us out of here."

The engines roared as the pilot punched the throttle, pulling up. Ulian winced as the straps bit into his shoulders, pinching his skin through the uniform. They were practically climbing straight up, the vessel rattling as it fought gravity to climb. The sky outside faded from blue to gray then gradually changed to black.

Golden lights streaked in the distance, drop ships plunging toward the Earth. Ulian scowled, well aware that meant ground troops. They were throwing their people into the battle as quickly as possible without regard to the ground defenses that might blow their troop transports straight out of the sky.

I feel like I'm missing something. Ulian turned to his tablet, tapping into the tactical battle communication network. He found the Fortitude and established a link to their bridge. "Torqua? This is Ulian. Do you read me?"

"Not in the battle yet?" Torqua's voice boomed in Ulian's earpiece. "You always were quick to get to meetings. Lucky I stayed behind to start facing this threat. We've already engaged one of the destroyers. Should make short work of him. How long before the Stalwart can contribute to this battle?"

Ulian clenched his fist before answering. "This isn't a competition. But that's not why I'm talking to you. Something else is going on. They wouldn't just throw people away. Have you detected a pattern to the attack? Some purpose beyond harassing us while we try to plan our own assault?"

"They are terrorists, Ulian. They don't have any sort of real plan. They're madmen and you know it. This shouldn't be any sort of surprise to you. When we take prisoners, and undoubtedly we will, we'll learn that they're little more than pawns thrown at us in a flailing effort to prevent their own demise."

"Torqua ... you learned better than that." Ulian sighed. "Come on, man! Think! I just saw troop transports entering Earth's atmosphere. Why would they risk those men's lives without a plan?"

"Because they are led by fools. I heard that disgraced officer Trall Derkon joined them. If he planned this operation, we should make short work of it. Remember when we fought him in the games back at the academy? Nothing to be concerned about whatsoever." Torqua chuckled. "Anyway, I have to go. We're fighting here." The line went dead.

Ulian winced as the shuttle shook from a heavy blow. At first he thought they hit something but then he realized it must've been an energy blast. "What was that? What hit us?"

"A fighter," Eyros replied. The automatic turret started blasting away overhead. Every time it turned, the scrape of metal echoed in the cabin. "We're holding him off and we're nearly to the Stalwart."

"Damn it." Ulian brought Morala back on the com. "It seems I might need an escort after all. The Tol'An were far more expeditious with their attack force than anticipated."

"Yes, sir," Morala replied. "I haven't seen them use these tactics before. They're charging us, blowing through pickets and moving toward the planet. One of their destroyers was already taken out but they're not slowing down. What do you think they hope they can accomplish?"

"If they're desperate, they might be trying to destroy the Trindishas. That would end things pretty fast for us." Ulian scowled out the window as a number of smaller ships streaked by them. "Better get someone here in a hurry. We'll be to you soon but I'd rather not limp into the hangar if at all possible."

"I've got three pilots on their way right now," Morala replied. "I'm also engaged with an enemy ship so we're going to have to perform some clever shield work to get you onboard. I'll have Viran coordinate with your ship so we can get this done with the least amount of exposure. Morala out."

Ulian shifted in his seat to look out the other window. Capital ships engaged off in the distance thousands of kilometers away. Weapons fire lit up the sky, winking in and out of existence as shields responded with brilliant lights. Streams of smoke from missiles came out in gray globes and objects entering the atmosphere turned red with heat.

Sparks blinked off to his left where fighters engaged one another, a wild melee of Pahxin ships meeting the Tol'An fighters. Human vessels moved in to assist, the smaller destroyer classes that were not FTL capable, but still packed a good punch. They were the ones that held off the Tol'An during the first assault before the Gnosis got involved.

"This is going to be rough," Eyros said. "Hang on tight, sir. I see our escorts on scan but there's a fight between us and them. It'll take some flying to get through this."

"Do you need my help with anything?"

"You might want to take manual control of the turret. A human touch definitely outweighs the computer every time."

I haven't done that in a while. Ulian popped off his safety belt, tapping the panel to bring the seat down from the ceiling. It fell into place and he mounted the gun, riding it back up into the roof of the shuttle. Lights flashed on around him as a screen flickered to life, providing him with a high definition video feed of the surrounding area.

Taking the controls, he moved to the left and right, acclimating to the feel of how it moved. The first full turn made him a little dizzy but he shook it off, drawing a deep breath for the action to come. They were flying right through a brawl between allied pilots and the Tol'An invaders. Friend or foe engaged, red triangles representing applicable targets.

Ulian pulled the trigger, energy beams tearing through the dark of space. Beginner's luck made him nearly catch his first target but a quick climb saved them from a direct hit just above the rear thrusters. He tried to lead the next one, loosing a couple of quick bursts but each resulted in a clean miss.

The shuttle began to rock about, taking evasive maneuvers as stray attacks came deadly close to catching them on the sides. Ulian shot back but he ultimately only provided suppressive fire, keeping opponents away from assaulting their vessel. Then, he got lucky, blasting one of the Tol'An vessels directly in the nose.

Shields went bright then shattered. The nose buckled, twisting all the way to the cockpit. He saw the pilot get sucked out just before the ship exploded in a great orange globe, scattering debris in all directions.

Ulian smiled to himself though he couldn't take much pride in the act considering how poorly he'd done to that point. Three enemy ships closed on them. He fired, this time without any direction at all, just to keep them away. His blasts flew past them as they evaded. When they returned fire, his pilot responded but it was only a matter of time before they'd be hit.

"Can you shake them?" Ulian asked.

"I'm working on it, sir!" Eyros shouted back.

The shuttle started shaking as at least three blows caught them from behind. Ulian glared at the scanner, prepared to ask their escorts what exactly they were doing when two allied ships buzzed not even thirty feet above the shuttle. They laid into the pursuing vessels, scattering their formation and buying Ulian's pilot some breathing room.

"Stalwart, come in," Eyros spoke in a firm voice. "We're coming in. I need you to drop the shields before we get there. What's the timing?"

Ulian didn't hear the rest of the conversation. He continued shooting, pot shots at the enemies swarming around them. He had no idea the Tol'An could field such a force, let alone bring it to bear in such a tactically sound manner. Torqua must've been wrong about Trall because the man pulled off a brilliant surprise attack.

Depending on how it went in the next thirty minutes, he might even pull off a victory if his troops he sent to the surface made it to their objective. Ulian still felt as if there were more to the plan than met the eye. Hammering the defenses of a planet worked with available reinforcements or an auxiliary attack force.

The Tol'An didn't have access to that sort of thing. So what were they relying on?

"Hang on tight!" Eyros yelled again, dragging Ulian out of his reverie. "I can't evade this incoming attack!"

The shuttle shook again, this time rattling so hard Ulian was convinced they'd been destroyed. He wondered how long it would take for the turret capsule to be compromised, sending him into deep space. His monitor screen flickered and his scanner showed they took a rocket to the thrusters.

Eyros guided the ship in on momentum alone, kicking in retro-thrusters just a second before they entered the Stalwart. The bottom of their craft scraped across the deck, nearly colliding with the wall on the opposite side. Ulian got jostled about, cracking his head against the side of the turret compartment.

He rubbed the bump, tapping the panel to free himself from the hatch. "We made it," Eyros grunted. "We're ... onboard ..."

"You okay?" Ulian opened the door to the cockpit. Eyros clung to his stomach, his flight suit coated in blood. "Oh my ... okay, you're going to be okay, son. Hold on!" He tapped his tablet. "I need a medic on this shuttle immediately! We have a wounded man here! I repeat, medics report to the hangar right now!"

He looked toward the rear of the ship, eyes widening when he noted the ramp was gone. The fact the turret capsule remained sealed was the only reason he survived. Landing the ship safely at all took incredible luck and a lot of skill. Ulian put his hand on Eyros's shoulder, squeezing it.

"I'm not leaving you until the medics get here," Ulian said. "Don't you dare die on me. I don't want to have to give you an order on that. We don't have a lot of flyers like you and I refuse to lose the one who saved my life today, you understand?" He gave the man a chance to respond. When he didn't, Ulian raised his voice. "I said do you understand?"

"I ... do ..." Eyros grunted. He grit his teeth. "I'm not sure ... I can ... do this ... sir ..."

"You'd better!" Ulian got back on his com. "Where's my medic?"

"We're in the hangar now, sir!" A voice replied. "We're boarding the shuttle now!" Three people pounded into the vessel, rushing toward him. They were carrying a couple of medical kits and shooed him aside. "We've got this, sir. We'll get him to the medical bay right away. Are you injured?"

"Negative." Ulian backed away. "Don't you dare die on me, Eyros! I'll be checking on you personally and I expect to hear good things!"

"Yes, sir!" Eyros shouted. The medics went to work on him.

Ulian left the shuttle, reaching out to Morala. "I'm on board now and en route to the bridge. Get us moving toward the action. I want to be in position to start fighting the second we're there. Also, I want to get Captain Bradford on the line. The Gnosis might already be engaged, but we're going to provide some support for his shuttle on its way up."

"Yes, sir," Morala said. "That looked like a scary ride, sir."

"You have no idea," Ulian muttered. "Just get us underway. We've got a skirmish to win."

Chapter 5

Throughout the trip to the medical bay, Cassie had to fight hard to keep her wits about her, staring at the floor to avoid freaking out. When they finally arrived, Vincent was waiting. She hurried over to him, throwing her arms about his neck. He gripped her tightly, keeping her close.

"I have to go to the briefing," Desmond said. "You can wait here with her. Make sure she and Gil are okay."

"I'm on it." Vincent escorted her to a bed where she sat down. "Hey, you're going to be okay. They said that Gil's just sleeping. It's not really a coma ... just a very deep slumber."

Cassie nodded her head, still staring into space.

"Talk to me, hon. Are you in there?"

"Yes ..." Cassie lifted her head, looking into his eyes. "I feel like ... like I'm in a dream. You know how everything looks foggy and weird? I'm just ... stuck ... sort of ... lost. I don't know how to describe it beyond that. I'm floating ... kind of."

"Let me help you get comfortable." Vincent lowered her onto the bed and she stared up at the ceiling, resting her hands on her stomach. Time passed but she didn't know how much. She heard voices around her. Someone scanned her but she didn't move. Just remained staring in place.

An alarm caught her attention, a constant buzzing from somewhere in the hall. Red lights flashed nearby. Cassie knew what it meant. Someone was attacking the base. Again. The last time it happened was the militia Christina was investigating. Who would have the nerve to do it again?

Desmond burst into the room. "Vincent! We have to go. Tol'An just entered orbit. They've got a lot of ships up there."

"But ..." Vincent sighed. "Cassie, I have to go. Will you be okay here?"

Cassie felt her faculties returning. Some of the mist started to lift from her mind. She nodded emphatically. "Yes. Go ... I'll ... I'll be fine. I'm ... sorry I can't go with you. I should be there."

"You'll be with us when we take the fight to them." Vincent hurried after Desmond. "I promise! Just get well while we're gone! We'll see you soon!"

Cassie watched them go, turning her attention to Gil. The Pahxin archaeologist did look sound asleep. She thought they might have to do something to help him, something more than let him linger there but she didn't know what. Especially with what was happening around them. Any sort of procedure would have to wait until the danger had been dealt with.

Wait. A thought dawned on her. *Tammy was here. I hope to hell she got out.* Cassie checked her tablet, trying to establish a connection with her sister's terminal. It took several pings before she finally answered. "Hello? Cassie?" The fear in her voice was like stabbing daggers. "What's happening here?"

"Did you not get out of the base yet?" Cassie asked. "Are you still here?"

"Yes … I was in a waiting room near the tarmac. They were getting a passenger shuttle ready for a bunch of us but then the alarms went off and now we're stuck here."

"Damn it!" Cassie moved toward the door. One of the medics tried to stop her.

"Ma'am, you can't leave! You've been checked in."

"I'm busy," Cassie replied. "I need to get to my sister."

"But … you can't!" He turned to one of the others. "Doctor, please! Can you help?"

Cassie spun on them. "Listen to me, all of you. Yes, that was a trying experience but I can't just sit around here hoping I'll get better over the next twenty or thirty minutes while we're under attack. Now, you can either back the hell off or I can ensure you wished you did. Either way, I'm walking out this door and ensuring innocent lives are not lost in this conflict."

"If she's that feisty," one of the other doctors spoke up, "let her go. We have people who can't walk around on their own right now."

"Thank you." Cassie hurried out the door, jogging for the civilian waiting area. "Are you still on the line Tammy?"

"I am, but there are ships or something coming down from the sky, Cassie. I can see these weird streams of smoke. A whole bunch of them."

"Okay, I want you to come back into the base. Head down the hall toward the cafeteria."

"They're not letting us leave!" Tammy shouted. "Wait! What're you doing? I'm talking to my sister on that!" Her voice went distant. "Come on! That's my tablet! Leave it alone! Hey! Don't!" The line went dead a moment later.

Cassie pushed herself, moving to a full run. Explosions outside rumbled the ground, tiny tremors that indicated a distance of half a mile or so. She figured they were landing vehicles, crafts depositing troops from the invading force. Were they Tol'An? Pahxin? Someone knew? Or just another bunch of human traitors?

Distant gunfire caught her attention, automatic rifles popping off maybe two hundred yards away. Cassie cursed the fact she didn't have a weapon of her own but she figured one wouldn't be hard to acquire from the guards when she arrived for the civilians. Why they hadn't been moved to safety was beyond her.

Rounding the corner, she plowed into a heavy crowd taking up the hallway. The people seemed to be panicking, unsure exactly what to do with themselves. They were the civilian contractors, the technicians, and engineers without the military experience to maintain discipline in light of the attack.

Cassie shoved through them but had to pause finally, shouting to attract their attention. "Listen!" Most of them went silent, giving her some space. "You all need to move out of here in an orderly fashion! The enemy isn't here yet. Get to the shelters near the center of Gamma Alpha and await further instructions but you *cannot* remain here!"

"Who the hell are you to tell us what to do?" A random voice called from the back.

"I'm Special Agent Cassandra Alexander of the AIA," Cassie replied. "And I do not want to have to bring guards in here to escort you but I will. You'd be wasting valuable resources if you force my hand. So please, for your own safety and to ensure this passageway is clear for official business, get moving!"

The people surged suddenly, practically carrying her with them as they headed off. Cassie fought her way through them, shoving hard until she broke free. Only a few stragglers remained but she ignored them, instead running for her destination again.

A voice crackled on the speaker overhead, one of the men from the control room. "Attention, all civilian personnel should report to the shelters immediately."

Cassie groaned. *You're a little late*. Another explosion sounded in the distance, this one far closer than the last. She checked her tablet, bringing up a scan program while on the run. Her head started aching, probably a side effect from being under with the Orb for so long. She fought through the pain, slowing down as she approached the corridor leading outside.

A soldier stepped in her way, his rifle held over his chest. "Whoa there, lady! Where do you think you're going?"

"I'm here for Tammy Alexander." Cassie tapped her tablet to bring up her ID and showed it to him. "I'm AIA. The rest of the people here can come with me too. I'll take them into the shelter."

"I have orders for the nonworking personnel to remain here," he replied. "I can't let you take them."

"Then we've got a problem," Cassie said, "because I'm not letting these people remain so close to where the action is likely to take place. Who's your CO? I'll call them right now but we don't really have time for this."

The guard looked at her then glanced over his shoulder. He frowned. "They were just trying to catch a shuttle out of here ... it's pretty messed up to leave them here."

"I agree," Cassie replied. "But we're still wasting time."

He sighed, then stepped aside. "Go ahead."

Cassie burst through, pausing just inside the room. Tammy stood, an expression of terror etched on her face. "You made it!" She hurried over and hugged her sister. "I can't believe you made it!"

"Of course I did." Cassie patted her on the back once. "We have to go now." She turned to the others, four men dressed in business suits. "All of you are going to want to come with me. I'll get you to safety."

"Deeper into the base?" One asked. "That doesn't seem safer."

"They're going to be fighting right out there." Cassie gestured to the door leading outside. "If you want to risk the fact they might get inside and have no compunctions about shooting you, that's your business. I for one would rather you get your ass in gear and follow me so we can avoid that."

They looked amongst one another before standing, falling in behind her. Cassie turned to the guard. "Where can I get a gun? I was in the middle of a meeting and couldn't arm myself before I got here."

"There's an armory on the way." The guard showed her the path to it on his tablet. "Do you know the area?"

"I do." Cassie checked her scanner. Five vehicles landed in the immediate area and there were at least sixty troops moving on the base. Something was trying to jam her scanner though, interfering with good numbers. "You'd better get some reinforcements up here, soldier. I think they might get into the courtyard this time."

"I will. Good luck!"

Cassie gestured for the others to follow her, leading them back down the hallway. They shouted questions at her but she shushed them with a wave of her hand. Shots outside became faster paced, rattling off in rapid succession. Fighters passed by overhead, low enough to make the walls rattle.

Those trailing behind Cassie started really panicking. Tammy grabbed her arm, pulling hard. "Are we going to die in here?"

"No," Cassie spoke firmly. She stopped in front of the armor where two men stood guard with rifles. A third lingered nearby, trying to look busy but failing miserably. They could've locked the door and joined the fighting. "I'm Senior Agent Cassandra Alexander. I need a weapon."

"Um ... yes, ma'am." The guard on the left answered her. He didn't seem to care about whether she had the credentials or not. He just stepped aside.

Cassie approached the third wheel. "You, I need you to escort these people to the shelter right now."

"Absolutely!" The man smiled like she'd just told him he won the lottery. He waved at the others to come with him. "Come on! I can get us there in no time. I have a shortcut that should keep us *away* from the conflict."

Tammy tapped Cassie's shoulder. "I don't want to go with that idiot, I want to stay with you."

"You can," Cassie replied. "I'm going to grab a weapon and I'll take you somewhere safe." She watched the others rush off. The two guards stared longingly after them. "You two should probably lock this up after I get what I need and find a way to help. If your CO learns you sat here during the fight, I doubt you'll be happy with the results."

They exchanged a glance. The one on the right shrugged. "Better to be in trouble than dead."

Cassie shook her head, entering the room. Most of the weapons had already been allocated but she grabbed a small submachine gun, some extra magazines, and a sidearm. Strapping the smaller weapon to her hip, looking around for anything else that might be of value. The grenade crates were empty and all the body armor was gone.

I guess this is it, Cassie thought. She stepped back into the hall, addressing the guards. "At least lock this door and leave the area. If someone gets this far, we'll have bigger problems than a few stray pistols falling into enemy hands."

She grabbed Tammy's hand and dragged her off down the hall, taking a different turn than the guard leading the other civilians did. They were heading for operational control. Cassie figured if she was going to contribute to the fight, that would be the best way. The others had already returned to the Gnosis.

And flying around up there would be insane right now anyway. Cassie glanced at her scanner. A full-on brawl was taking place nearby. Anti-aircraft guns barked near the perimeter, rapid-fire shots competing with the alarm blaring overhead. *I'm pretty sure everyone knows we're under attack. They could probably shut off the siren.*

"Where're we going?" Tammy asked.

"We need to help," Cassie said. "And we'll be able to get something done down in control. Unfortunately, it's pretty far away. We'll be moving for a bit. Just ... stick close. I don't foresee any trouble. Not for us. But I don't know how thorough this attack is or who we're even fighting."

"Isn't there someone you can ask?"

"No reason right now," Cassie replied. "Everyone I know is busy anyway. We'll get our own answers. You have to trust me. Can you do that?"

Tammy nodded emphatically. "This is your world. I'm not about to argue with you about how to survive in it."

"Good." Cassie sighed. *At least that's one less thing to worry about. Now, to get us where we need to be with the least amount of trauma. That's the trick.* The scanner indicated they were approaching a side entrance. It may have been compromised given where the enemy ships landed.

If so, a real fight could be going on near there ... or enemy agents may have entered the base. Scans didn't show who they were facing so she didn't know what kind of opposition to expect. Either way, they didn't have a choice about their destination and who they fought didn't really matter if a brawl became inevitable. *We'll cross that gun battle when we get to it.*

***

General Trall stood on the bridge of his battleship, watching the operation unfold on the main screen. Eighty percent of the deployed soldiers made it to the surface of the planet. He wondered where their human allies were and why they hadn't joined the fray. Their own resources may not have been up to the rapid deployment task.

Still, the Tol'An attack seemed like it would be more than a match for the paltry defenses they were facing on the surface. Orbit was another matter entirely. The Pahxin committed a large number of vessels to the planet and they were delivering quite the pounding. Chances of them stopping the mission were slim to none.

After all, they couldn't guess at the purpose Ezria had in mind. Trall found it shocking but he obeyed. The grand scheme of things, the vision of their future, was not his to know. He merely embraced the word of his master and enacted it. He refused to become like Gizan, an out of favor outlaw, hunted throughout the galaxy.

No, he would maintain his honor and fulfill his mission. Without their reinforcements, additional risk had been introduced into the situation but Trall tried to mitigate it by sending additional fighters to the surface to provide cover. He wondered why the military forces of the Pahxin converged on the base.

It didn't make a great deal of tactical sense other than to protect the Trindishas but wouldn't they have been better off moving them to a more secure location? Trall knew they were sentimental but allowing the humans to dictate defensive measures seemed foolhardy to say the least.

These pathetic creatures didn't know how to handle themselves in space. Their survival relied solely on luck, a concept which had finally run out for them. This attack, this assault, would not go down as the last one had. Trall did not underestimate their tenacity or their fortune. He brought an overwhelming number of troops to crush them once and for all.

And once they concluded their business there, they could turn their attention to the Pahxin homeworld. That would be the real prize in Trall's mind. The one that he had vested interested in. If anyone deserved to be destroyed for their impertinence, their arrogance and pride, it was those self-righteous military bastards.

You never should have drummed me out, Trall thought. *I'll make you all pay for that soon enough.*

***

Desmond and Vincent arrived at the landing field, pausing just inside the door to look out. An aerial battle took place roughly a mile to the south, ships flying in and out of each other in dramatic dogfights. Anti-aircraft guns fired at incoming vessels dropping from orbit, probably troop transports based on how large their vapor trails were.

Marines shouted all around them, charging the walls. Those already in position fired at the ground, blasting away at incoming ground troops. The carnage gave them both pause.

"We have to get up there," Desmond said. "We've got escorts standing by but I think the two of us shouldn't go together."

"I agree," Vincent replied. "At least one of us has to make it to the ship alive." He paused. "And this must be the most morbid conversation we've ever had."

"Yeah, I'm not loving it." Desmond looked around. "Just getting to the shuttles might prove to be an adventure. There's not even a guard at the door right now."

"They're all holding back the tide." Vincent looked about. "I say we wait for the next ship to pass us overhead and make a run for it. I'll take the ship on the right, you grab the one on the left. Sound good?"

Desmond shrugged. "As good as any other plan." A moment later, the rumble of engines came toward them from the north. The whine of the thrusters didn't sound like one of their vessels. The double A guns swiveled and started blasting away. An explosion made both men stumble back into the base.

When the chunks of ship impacted the ground, a secondary boom washed the area in a wash of heat intense enough to make breathing difficult. Desmond moved back to the door cautiously, sighing when he saw their shuttles had been obliterated. The fires rose up a good thirty feet in the air.

"We have a big problem." Desmond waited for Vincent to see what he was talking about. "How're we going to get up there now?"

"We can get to the fighters in the hangar," Vincent suggested. "We're both qualified still."

"Yeah, qualified doesn't necessarily mean combat competent." Desmond considered the idea for a moment. It might've been the only way to get into the fight and at least they'd be able to defend themselves. "Alright, so if we do this, we're going to divert all power to our defenses and make like a bat out of hell straight for the Gnosis."

"Understood."

"And we'll still try to find an escort." Desmond scowled, glancing at the hangar. It was two hundred yards from their position, requiring them to run over open ground. "That's a bit of a trek. Stay close to the building and don't stop. You got it? I have a bad feeling about going out there. It's going to be crazy."

"Nothing's easy, sir." Vincent patted Desmond. "I'll take the lead. You ready?"

"As I'll ever be, I guess." The two of them dashed from their cover, running along the side of the building. After a dozen yards, they were sprinting as guns exploded all around them, explosions shaking the ground and walls. Desmond saw more ships coming in out of the corner of his eye, landing hard near the base.

This is a full-scale invasion. But what's their objective? This doesn't seem like they want to take the Orbs. Desmond's eyes widened but he didn't have time to voice his concerns. They had to keep moving, keep running the whole time. *They are here to destroy them. To blow them up. Better no one have them than us.*

Concrete exploded into the air barely five feet away, blasted by automatic fire. Desmond raised his hand, flinching away from the debris as it showered them and clapped against the wall. He picked up the pace, casting a glance to the left. A section of the wall had been taken down. Invaders came through, pressing toward the main complex.

"They're through!" Desmond shouted. He tapped his com unit. "Bradford to control, do you copy? You've got a breach near the landing area! Repeat, incoming soldiers in the landing area. Respond!"

"We read you." The voice was indistinct, the sounds barely registering as words before they were cut off.

Vincent hustled into the hangar with Desmond close behind. Shadows blanketed them, darkness as the roof blocked out the sun. Six fighters were lined up with a couple of technicians hunkered down behind some metal crates. They came out when the two officers entered, moving toward the door to provide some cover.

"Hey, Stanford!" Vincent clapped one of them on the shoulder, a burly man with a thick beard and grease stained blue jumpsuit. "Fancy meeting you here, huh?"

"You're lucky to be alive after running across that field," Stanford said. "What brings you both here?"

One of the other technicians started shooting, firing a couple short bursts outside.

"We need to get to the Gnosis," Vincent replied. "Mind if we grab a couple of these fighters?"

"Those two are ready," Stanford pointed. "But they only have blasters. No missiles. If you're going up there for some action, you'll need to stick to guns."

"Fair enough," Vincent said. "Got some helmets in them?"

"Yeah, hopefully they fit." Stanford led the way to the ships. "Climb aboard and I'll get you moving. You probably won't get much in the way of a taxi run but you shouldn't need it. How long has it been since you've flown one of these things anyway?"

"A while." Vincent grinned at Desmond. "Longer for him."

"Yeah, yeah." Desmond boarded his ship, grabbing the helmet from the seat. He pulled it on, tapping the code to get the reactor online. "You got me on com, Commander?"

"I hear you," Vincent said. "We can't leave without putting down some suppressive fire on the invaders though, don't you think?"

"I thought about it." Desmond checked the thrusters. They showed ready to go. "There are a lot of pilots up here. I don't want to get in the way. We'll tell them what's going on and support from the ship. Follow my lead. You ready?"

"Ready."

Desmond pressed the throttle forward, leading his ship out of the hangar. The marines engaged in a firefight just outside, tearing through the invading force. They were holding them back, but only barely. If reinforcements didn't arrive for them, they'd be in some serious trouble.

"Bradford to Gnosis, do you read?"

"This is Zach. I'm holding position in orbit waiting for your command."

"Vincent and I are on the way in fighters. I'm sure the marines are already poised for action but they need to get down here in a hurry. Have them report to the hangar immediately then send them in a shuttle to reinforce Gamma Alpha. The invading force has pushed into the courtyard and will arrive in the building at any moment."

"Understood."

Desmond accelerated, pulling up as he moved outside. The bottom thrusters gave him the lift he needed to launch in the air, sending him upward at a forty-five-degree angle. As the vessel gained speed, he had to juke the controls to the left, narrowly avoiding contact with an enemy fighter.

Vincent came up to his left as they high tailed it to break atmosphere. The com net went crazy, chatter from every battle occurring all around them. Pilots on the surface and in space competed with the ground crews. They all seemed to be on the same channel but someone in control fought to move them about, grouping them up.

A couple stray shots caught Desmond on the shields. He resisted the urge to veer away, glancing down at his scanner. It took him a moment to find the right screen. Sweat broke on his back. The red blips were moving away, two green ones came racing up from behind. The com chatter died down until only one voice came through.

"This is Lieutenant Darnell coming up on your six. I'm guessing you two aren't enemy hijackers hoping to make a quick getaway. Identify yourselves."

"Captain Desmond Bradford and Commander Vincent Bowman. We're on our way to the Gnosis to take command there. Darnell, are we clear to orbit or is there more action going on up here than we know about?"

"The primary fight's happening down below," Darnell said. "You might find a few guys on their way down here to cause some trouble though. Be on your guard." He paused. "We have to get back to the action. Good luck, gentlemen though I hope you don't need it. This is one hell of a day."

The allied ships pulled away, plunging back toward the surface.

"He's not kidding," Vincent added. "Control cleared the line. Looks like Admiral Reach is on."

"Admiral, this is Captain Bradford, do you copy?"

"I do, where are you?" Reach shouted the words. "All hell's breaking loose down here so I hope to God you got on board the Gnosis."

"Negative, we're on our way," Desmond said, "but we're sending some marine reinforcements down right away. They should be there soon."

"Thanks, I guess we can be glad we sent a force to take care of those traitors. According to Dulain, they'd probably be here right now. Some signal came in to warn someone on the base. So I guess we've got that going for us right now."

"Damn." Desmond paused as the sky turned gray. They were on the verge of breaking orbit. "Sir, I need to go. We're almost to the Gnosis. I'll talk to you when we're on board and moving into position. Keep me informed if there's anything else we can do. Bradford out." He switched over to Vincent. "You ready for this mad dash?"

"As I'll ever be, I guess. Scans show we've got quite the crowd between us and the ship. Can't say I'm excited about that dash."

"Yeah, well ... it'll be your excitement for the week." Desmond took a deep breath as they left the atmosphere, the sky turning black with only stars sparkling out in the distance. Without wind resistance, the ship handled in a totally different manner, responding instantly to any stick motion. *I have to get used to this.*

A battle raged out ahead of them, Pahxin and human ships meeting the Tol'An invaders. Energy beams lit up the darkness, flashing brightly enough to reveal the source of the attacks, giving away their rapid movements. Desmond turned to his scanner to get a better look, watching as ships flipped and spun in impossible maneuvers, all in the course of combat.

"Not that I needed it," Desmond said, "but I have a newfound respect for our pilots. Jesus Christ."

"And we get to fly right down the middle of all that noise." Vincent chuckled. "Well, we could also go around but I've plotted the course and it would add several minutes to the trip."

"Bradford to Gnosis, come in."

"Zach here, sir. What's your position?"

"We're in orbit but maybe you could come meet us halfway. There's a pretty big fight we'd have to get through and I'd rather be out there for as little time as possible. You guys able to pull away from what you're doing?"

"The real action is a ways off," Zach replied. "I can break from where we're at. I'm sending you some rendezvous coordinates. See you there in a moment."

"That's something." Desmond squared his shoulders. "Alright, Vincent. Let's make this happen, huh? Time to see what we're really made of."

***

Christina entered the briefing room, finding Dulain sitting alone with his tablet. She paused just inside the door. The building kept shaking from random explosions and raging conflict. Aircraft screamed by overhead, emitting booms loud enough to make ears pop, the roar of their engines lingering long after they left.

"Comfortable?" Christina asked. "I thought you would be in the control room by now."

"No point," Dulain replied. "They're running this battle. I'm locking down security corridors."

"Don't you think their people are on that?"

Dulain shook his head. "No, or I wouldn't be doing it." He paused. "They clearly want the Orbs but the scary thing is, if you look at their landing pattern, they're not here to collect anything. I think they want to blow them up. If I'm right, this battle is a lot more important than anyone realizes."

"If all four of those go up ..." Christina pinched the bridge of her nose. "We'd lose half the continent."

"Exactly." Dulain smirked. "See why I'm here?"

"What can I do to help?"

"I'm not sure. Did we apprehend the traitor?"

"Yes, he was a major who escorted the Pahxin ambassadors on their first visit. Apparently, they'd been compromised and as a result, this guy got involved. He supposedly has connections with some ass who runs a mercenary unit. That's who our people are fighting out there right now."

"Figures. What were they, cousins?"

"I don't know, probably in-laws. We won't know any more than that until we can properly interrogate him and considering what's going on, that might be a while." Christina approached, looking over his shoulder. "Did Cassie go up to the Gnosis?"

"No, she was in the medical bay. I doubt she left."

"I'm going to contact her. See if she can get in the game." Christina stepped away, engaging her com. "Agent Alexander, come in."

"Christina? Hey! I'm glad to hear from you. Where are you?"

"We're in the big briefing room," Christina said. "Are you still in medical?"

"Negative. I'm making my way to control. We're sort of taking the long way considering how jammed up the hallways are."

"Who's we?" Christina asked.

"I have a civilian in tow. What's your status?"

Christina glanced at Dulain before answering. "We're locking doors. Trying to prevent the enemy from getting to the Orbs."

"Are they Tol'An?"

"Yep." Christina sat down. "The good news is we probably prevented their allies from joining the battle by attacking them first. Of course, that left us a little light on defenses. At least for now. All those Pahxin military folks up there are getting involved. Shouldn't be long before we get an influx of ground forces."

"Okay, if you think of something we can do …"

"You should get your civilian to a shelter," Christina interrupted. "You can't drag someone around like that."

Dulain cleared his throat. "We have a problem but Cassie seems to be in a position to solve it. One of the doors isn't responding to automated messages but she's close enough that she should be able to get over there and take care of it manually. I'm pinging her tablet near there at least. I'm sending her some coordinates. Have her get over there ASAP."

"We have a task for you," Christina said. "I'm not sure how dangerous it is or if it's a good idea to bring your civvy but we need a door locked down manually. Can you take care of it?"

"Yeah, I see where it is. We're nearly there now. Shouldn't be a big deal."

"Who is the civilian you're with anyway?"

"Um …" Cassie paused. "My sister."

"I'm guessing she's regretting her decision to come visit you," Christina said. "Of course, if we fail here it won't matter where someone is on the planet. Earth will be done. Get that door locked. I'm going to check on the defenses around the Orbs. Dulain will coordinate us from here."

"You've got it," Dulain said. "I'll start up a secure, private line. Damn it!" He sighed. "Some of them have entered the base. Be careful, guys. They're going to move quick but probably don't know how to get where they're going. You could encounter them anywhere as they navigate the corridors. I'll track them the best I can."

"Thanks." Christina checked her weapon, ensuring a round was chambered. Satisfied, she headed for the door. "Least we won't be bored during this little invasion. Oh well. Back into the fray then."

Chapter 6

Captain Kent led seven men down into the bowels of the militia base. He prepared himself for impact, for being shot by an energy weapon that would tear through his armor and kill him instantly. Still he pressed on, swallowing his fear while keeping an eye on the scanner on the lower left of his HUD.

Dashwood paced behind him, two stairs up. They had to go down single file as the armor was too wide for anything else. Stealth was out of the question. Every footfall sounded like a forklift crashing into a wall. Eight of them doing it made a cacophonous sound. Anyone down below knew exactly when the marines would come out.

Kent paused for half a moment to look at the scan. If he darted to the left, he'd get to some cover though he wasn't sure what exactly he'd be hiding behind. It could've been metal, rock or grate. Depending on which, he'd find himself exposed or safe. Any enemies waiting to shoot at them must've wanted something more than his legs.

"I'm going in," Kent called to the others, dashing into the room then throwing himself to the left. He found himself in a small alcove, probably a guard post under normal circumstances. There was an exact copy of the space opposite him. Both sported a desk and a couple terminals. "Dashwood, cut right when you get in here."

Dashwood complied, hurrying into the room. The moment he showed himself, a beam slapped the wall only inches above his head. He ducked, returning fire before crouching in the cover. "Everyone stay back!" He shouted. "Get back up the stairs. They've got the area covered!"

Kent aimed his weapon, using the camera on top to get a look at the situation. A short hallway ended in what appeared to be another cargo space. *This stuff feeds the hangar down here. This is one of their supply routes.* He only saw one man out there but he felt certain the guy wasn't alone.

Another beam danced from that one enemy, hitting the wall just below his gun. He drew back with a curse.

"Just one that I saw," Kent said. "But I'm doubting it. Thoughts?"

"Rockets," Dashwood replied. "I'm all about hitting them hard."

"This place could come down!" Another beam hit the wall. "Screw it, you're right. Let's just do it." He brought up the targeting with his rockets, leaning out for a decent line of sight. Dashwood did the same. They fired together, dodging back into cover. The HUD scans showed the rockets streak through the hall, narrowly missing the walls as they barreled toward the crates.

A scream sounded moments before explosions rocked the building. Com chatter lit up, asking if they were okay. Rocks fell, massive stones collapsing until sunlight beamed into the room through the gathered smoke and dust. Kent looked out, peering into the room above them that had been battered by shuttle fire.

"That ... might've been overkill."

"No doubt, but it must've worked," Dashwood said. Another beam fired, this time at the stairs.

"You were saying?"

"Oh screw this!" Dashwood dashed from his cover, charging out into the open. Kent sighed, following after him. The others came pouring down the stairs, cutting down the hallway in rapid order.

More beams blasted at them from at least three different sources. One seared Kent's left shoulder, another caught one of his men in the chest and the third blasted Dashwood on his right hip, spinning him in place. He collapsed on the ground, rolling to his stomach to return fire.

The others opened up, their weapons barking in the confined space. Even with the hole in the ceiling, the sound was enough for Kent's helmet suppression to kick in full bore. He barely heard the pops of each round discharging. Red mist exploded behind one target, his limbs flailing as he danced backward.

One turned to run but Kent caught him in the lower back, nearly cutting him in half. The body collapsed so fast it was like something slapped it from above, pinning him to the floor in an instant. The final one aimed directly at Kent, smiling a split second before he pulled the trigger … and nothing happened.

The man's eyes went wide. He pulled the trigger again. Kent aimed his own gun at the man but before he could open his mouth, a rifle barked. The enemy's head snapped back, blood exploding from the back of his skull as he collapsed in a pool of gore. The weapon scattered away, skidding into the rocks.

"So much for prisoners," Kent muttered. He turned back to Dashwood. "Hey! How bad is it? You hurt?"

"I don't think so," Dashwood said. He rolled on his back. The armor was melted but no meat was visible. "I'm a little numb down there ... like being punched really god damn hard. Can you see the bone?"

"No," Kent replied. "Can you move it?"

He bent his knee, sucking breath through his teeth. "Well, it doesn't feel good but it must not be broken."

"Then get your ass up, we have to get down to the hangar." Kent hoisted him to his feet. He checked on the other men. Moll took the shot to the chest and though he hadn't died, he was out of action since breathing hurt. The other was already up and ready to go, stretching his arm. "Looks like we're good on that front."

"Let's get a look at these toys they were zapping at us with." Kent approached one of the high-tech weapons lying on the ground. The thing was barely the size of a submachine gun though the barrel was extra wide, accounting for the width of the beams they saw. "Jesus. That thing looks nasty."

"Too small to use with the armor," Dashwood said. "Looks open enough to bring the rest of the guys in."

"You're right." Kent got on the com, pausing to look at the hole in the ceiling. "You guys can catch up now if you're done mopping up. There's an entrance inside the building without using the stairs too. You won't have to go single file but hurry up. We're making the final push to the hangar and having you at our backs would be nice."

"We moving on?" Dashwood nodded. "Let's go, boys! Next hallway!"

They moved up, around the rocks and to a larger hallway. A heavy breeze rushed along, whistling as it cut through the grates. Kent checked the scan, frowning at the large number of enemy blips. He moved out, aiming his weapon as he went. He saw figures some hundred and fifty yards away, running away.

"They're fleeing alright," Kent said. He picked up the pace, moving into a brisk jog. "Shuttle three, are you in position to stop any traffic from this hangar?"

"I'm a little busy!" The pilot shouted back. They heard blaster fire rumbling the rocks all around them as heavy guns went off. Kent's scanner showed that some kind of power was surging over and over again, a fully automatic defensive emplacement. Another high-tech toy from the Tol'An no doubt. "This gun is all over my ass! Shuttle two, I need some help!"

Shit, I hope he can last until we get there. Kent broke into a sprint, firing his weapon as he ran. The first few bursts got lucky, tearing through the legs of some of his targets. Return fire filled him with some relief: conventional weapons this time. No more laser guns. *They left those people behind to delay us but what for?*

Where were these people going to go that they wouldn't be found again? Kent shoved the questions out of his mind. The others opened up as well. They started cutting through the enemy ranks, even as bullets tapped their armor, ricocheting off their torsos and arm pieces. That was what happened to the men topside: they didn't stand a chance with their gear.

"Grenade!" Dashwood's voice made the speaker crackle as he shouted. The marines dodged to the side, moving against the walls as the grenade went off. Tiny shards of metal popped in all directions at high enough velocity to stick *into* their power armor.

Kent held his arm up to defend his head, drawing back to see a dozen fragments stuck a quarter inch into the metal of his bracer. More grenades followed, half a dozen rolling near them. The marines hopped backward, using their jump jets to clear the detonation radius. As the ordnance went off, dust drifted down from the walls.

The enemy seemed to round a corner, taking themselves out of line of sight. It had to be the hangar. Scans saw another energy surge, this time not the weapons but engines from some kind of ship. Kent used his jump jets to buy some distance, hurling himself down the hall. He'd never tried something like that before and struggled to navigate, to avoid the walls and ceiling.

He couldn't slow down as he approached the corner, blowing past it and nearly slamming into the rocks at the end of the corridor. Men were loading up on troop transports. A couple fired at him but most sprinted straight for the safety of the ships. Five ships occupied the space, each of them firing up their engines.

Kent fired his remaining rockets into the room, the explosives whistling as they covered the short distance to their targets. Other marines arrived just as the first of his four attacks connected with one of the troop transports. The doors were not quite closed and they hadn't powered on any shields.

Metal buckled, the engines flared and a moment later went up in a massive explosion. The force knocked the marines backward into the wall, a section of hull plating burying itself in the wall only three feet from Kent's head.

Collateral damage from the blast nudged one of the other ships and it rocketed forward, slamming into the wall. It settled on the ground, lopsided as the landing gear failed and buckled. Smoke poured from the thrusters, the lights fading out.

One of the ships launched, pulling veering hard as it pulled away. The next tried to follow it but was rewarded with half a dozen rockets from some of the other marines. It started to climb then plunged toward the earth, fire streaming out of the rear. Fire from the destruction appeared briefly in front of the hangar then faded out.

The final ship was stuck behind the others but before Kent could say anything, the other marines arrived, plowing into it with a full salvo of missile fire. Dashwood shouted for everyone to take cover. Each of the soldiers dashed away from the carnage as the mountain itself seemed to respond with a massive quake.

Rocks started falling around them, larger boulders obscuring the path. Kent darted around them, using his jump jets once again to give him some speed. This time, he was far more reckless, bouncing off the ceiling, hitting the walls, and plowing through some of the smaller obstacles.

He risked a glance behind him. The tunnel was collapsing. Urgency filled his chest but he had only fifty yards to go to get back to the room with no ceiling. Other men rocketed past him. He pressed himself harder. Every time something fell, it made the whole world shake violently.

Kent hit his rockets just as he entered the room, flying straight up and through the destroyed ceiling. A moment later, he saw clear sky around him. Coming down swiftly, he landed clumsily, rolling several times before sliding to a halt. Others landed around him, some gracefully, some as poorly as he did.

Dashwood offered him a hand. "That was a hell of a thing, huh?"

Kent took his hand, though he wasn't ready to stand. He panted, trying to catch his breath. "You're way too calm about that."

"Hey, at least you didn't get shot." Dashwood looked at his arm. "Much."

"Shuttle three," Kent got on the com. "Are you okay? Is that gun taken care of?"

"Gun is down," another pilot answered. "Shuttle three took a direct hit and had to fall back. Ground forces on backup took some fire as well. They mopped up a few conventional forces trying to slip out."

"Mission complete," Kent said. "I need a casualty report. Rally at the center of the base for pickup. I'll call back to base to let them know. Good job, everyone. That was one hell of a brawl."

***

Mustang Squadron Leader Dennis Arden dodged an attempt to ram him, nearly colliding with a passing Pahxin ship. Traffic was thick in that particular sector as enemy ships attempted to dart for Earth. Those who remained in space attempted anything to keep the defending forces busy, including collision.

Charger lost two ships to Kamikaze style attacks and the Pahxin suffered casualties as well. The fight started suddenly, drawing all pilots from their leave to jump into the fight. Tol'An forces came on with a real purpose, bringing multiple capital ships and sending far more fighters than they'd seen in the past.

This seemed to be their full commitment, the sort of assault Dennis's people were planning to initiate against them. He couldn't imagine they thought they'd win, or even survive the engagement. A chilling thought told him they had no intention of getting back. They well may have come for a suicide run.

The Tol'An pilots certainly seemed to be.

Dennis pulled up and spun, letting an enemy ship pass beneath him. He pulled up hard, firing his weapons in several short bursts. He got his target, cutting through the weaker shields near the thrusters. It went up a moment later, just as several hits scattered over his own ship from the left.

He dove, a desperate maneuver to escape the barrage but it kept up until his shields were nearly depleted. The persistent attacker positioned itself behind him, firing again. Another series of shots blasted him, whittling down the shields to less than ten percent. Dennis pulled off more evasive maneuvers but he couldn't shake the man.

"Need some help over here," Dennis called. "Anyone able to get this guy off my ass?"

"I'm on it," Flight Lieutenant Shane Goring replied. "Oh, he's all over you."

"That's why I'm talking right now." Dennis climbed, pulling up so hard, he felt like he might pass out from the g-force. This time, his attacker couldn't match the motion, not to the same extreme. Checking scans, Dennis groaned. His opponent still had a reasonable firing solution and moved into position. "Any time, Shane!"

"Relax," Shane said.

The enemy fired, a clean miss.

"I'm not really in a position to relax, man!"

Light flashed behind Dennis, his scans going dark. He glanced over his shoulder as Shane joined him. "Your playmate was low on shields. Just had to catch up really fast."

"Appreciate the save." Dennis started to say something else but a message came in from the Gnosis.

"Mustang One," Zach Caplan said, "I need you to form an escort and immediately divert to the coordinates I've sent you for escort duty. Respond."

"Escort duty?" Dennis laughed. "You have got to be kidding!" He jogged his controls to the right, saving himself from an incoming missile. Defensive flying occupied his thoughts for a moment before he could continue the conversation. "In case you haven't noticed, it's a little rough up here."

"Understood," Zach said. "But Captain Bradford and Commander Bowman are incoming and I don't want them blown out of the sky because we were too busy to help them. Can you get there?"

"Damn it," Dennis muttered. "We're on our way." He switched over to Shane. "Two VIPs are making their way to the Gnosis. Let's make sure they get there. You ready for some crazy flying? The kind that will probably get us killed?"

"That's all we've been doing today," Shane said. "I'm in."

The two pilots pulled out of the fight, hitting their afterburners to pull away. No enemies chased them. There were far too many other pilots to mess with. The Pahxin alone probably could've handled them but the force was so large, it seemed prudent to put everyone in the air at the same time.

Better that than risk the base, the larger ships or civilian populations.

"Captain Bradford," Dennis called into the com. "Do you read me? This is Squadron Leader Dennis Arden. Please respond."

"This is Bradford," the voice came back, practically giving Dennis a heart attack. He checked and confirmed that the captain was on fast approach in a fighter. "Are you guys coming to help?"

"Flight Lieutenant Goring and I, yes," Dennis said. "Begging your pardon, sir, but was this the best option? Have you been behind a flight stick recently?"

"Been a few years," Bradford said. "But I'm remembering some things. I'd rather not have to get in a fight though if it's all the same to you."

"Perfectly understand." Dennis swallowed hard, checking the scans. They would have to pass through some fringe enemy activity before they arrived at the ship. "We'll try to keep things as smooth as possible but there are enemies in the way. Um … just follow our lead I guess." He switched to a private com with Goring. "Can you believe this?"

"Nothing surprises me anymore," Goring replied. "I have to talk to them. Switching to open channel. Um … Captain? Pull your nose up by twenty degrees, please. Commander, follow suit. When we hit the afterburners, remember that it's going to be a real kick to the face. You'll want to fight the urge to pass out."

"Understood, Flight Lieutenant," Vincent said. "Thank you for the tip and we're ready to go."

"Let's do it." Dennis took a deep breath. "Engage afterburners now."

The thrusters engaged, pressing Dennis into his seat with that all too familiar force. Captain Bradford grunted over the line as he did the same. Neither of the officers would be used to such activity, certainly not in a combat situation. Shane's idea was sound: aim them at the Gnosis and have them go in a straight line.

That would leave Dennis and Shane to handle any incoming attackers.

As they raced ahead, scans picked up three incoming fighters on an intercept course. Dennis groaned internally. "I'm sure you guys see them. They're heading straight for us." He wondered why they would bother, what specifically would draw their attention to the four ships on the edge of the combat zone.

They must think we're important. A number of shuttles had made their way to larger ships. Maybe they realized some fighters might be picking up the slack. *Time to drive these guys off and buy them some time.* "Shane, break formation and draw their fire. I'll back you up. Captain Bradford, maintain heading and speed. You should be at the Gnosis in three minutes."

Dennis pulled away, banking to the left while Shane went for the right. They would come at the attackers from two angles. When he saw their attack pattern, he cursed under his breath. *They're on one of their damn ramming courses!* The three ships barreled straight for Bradford and Bowman, engaging their afterburners to pick up speed.

"Sorry, guys," Dennis said. "I know what I just told you but you're going to have to initiate some evasive maneuvers. These idiots aren't here to shoot you down. They want to ram you."

"Are you serious?" Vincent asked. "Christ, what's wrong with these people?"

Bradford replied, "they're playing what they think is the final game. I'm not surprised we're seeing this kind of behavior. We'll take care of ourselves, Dennis. Do what you have to do. Take them out."

"I'll do my best." Dennis checked the scans for distance. They were still out of effective range. He fired anyway, hopeful it might fend them off or at least startle them out of formation. The energy beams came close but the ships didn't so much as flinch. *Okay, so they're determined. Fantastic.*

Shane started shooting, he gained a little more ground than Dennis. He fired rapidly, continuous shots as he barreled toward his targets. The first one took a full spread of shots, exploding in a spectacular fashion, almost as if he didn't have his shields on at all. Scans indicated something else, a massive energy reading like a generator going critical.

The other two ships were moving swiftly enough to avoid any appreciable damage. It proved lucky for them that the destruction of their friend took a few brief moments or they might've been annihilated right along with him. *That would've been terribly convenient*, Dennis thought. *But what are they doing to their ships?*

"Do you have any idea what that is?" Dennis asked. "I haven't seen anything like it before."

"The shield generators," Vincent said. "They've got them running hot so that when they hit something, they'll cause more damage with their explosion. That's insidious. Shit, they're getting really close."

Bradford pulled up, spinning once before resuming his course. Vincent went the opposite direction, splitting the enemy forces as they each broke to follow one of the targets. Shane spun around, going after the one chasing the captain. Dennis moved to intercept the remaining vessel.

"These guys are desperate!" Bradford shouted. "He's firing!"

Dennis glanced, watching as the enemy ship took some shots. Bradford dove, initiating too severe of a maneuver. It got him out of the way, but he made some serious noise about it over the com. Shane was catching up, moving into a perfect firing solution behind the target. Just as the enemy tried to dive, it took a full blast of energy beams straight to the tailpipe.

It started spinning as the other thrusters engaged, tossing them in all directions before the vessel finally exploded just as spectacularly as the first.

"Get him back to the Gnosis!" Dennis called. "I've got this one!"

The final enemy tried to catch Vincent but he proved to have a little more finesse on his controls, keeping himself just out of harm's way with clever motions to the left and right. Dennis dropped in behind and fired, scoring a clean miss just below his target. This time, the enemy responded, climbing to avoid another attack.

"Bingo," Dennis said. "Commander, veer hard left and catch up with the captain. I'll drive this guy off."

Vincent complied. The pursuer tried to catch up, pulling around to follow. Dennis blasted him right on the side, though he was far too close. As his target exploded, Dennis flew straight through the fire, his shields repelling the debris. *Thank God they juiced those generators up or the pieces would've been too big to fly through.*

"That's the last of them," Dennis said. "Are we clear to the Gnosis?"

"We are," Shane said. "Their automated guns are online and should be able to provide cover the rest of the way."

"Nevertheless, we're going to escort them to the end." Dennis drew a deep breath. Only then did he take a look and note his shields had barely crawled back up to thirty-five percent. Flying through the destroyed ship brought him back down to twenty. *Lord, that was far closer than it needed to be.* "Captain, how're you guys doing?"

"That was more excitement than we wanted," Desmond said, "but we made it. Great job, both of you and thanks. We appreciate the help."

"No problem." Dennis turned to his scanner, picking where they'd go next in the fight. They would rejoin the other human ships in fending off the fighters, trying to keep more larger ships from entering the Earth's atmosphere. That was their lot in life for the foreseeable future, but at least they kept two flag officers alive.

If nothing else, we have that victory. Phew.

***

"We have to make a detour," Cassie said. "Shouldn't take us long." She checked her tablet for the fasted path. "Yeah, no problem at all. Just a few minutes out of our way and we'll have kept this place safe. Come on."

"Wait!" Tammy grabbed her arm. "What's happening anyway? Who are we dealing with? What enemy is this? Are they aliens? And what're you defending? I don't understand any of this, Cassie! What is it that you even do? You've never made it clear and this ... this seems a lot more dangerous than what I thought!"

"We don't have time to discuss it right now." Cassie pulled her along and they got moving. "I'm with intelligence. You knew that meant clandestine stuff."

"You were an analyst I thought! A computer person for God's sake!" Tammy moved after her, still complaining. "Now you're carrying around some machine gun and we're going off to do something crazy! I don't like it! Can you just be honest with me? What is it you really do and how long have you done it?"

"I'm an agent," Cassie said. "And that doesn't mean just hanging around behind a computer terminal. I've learned how to do all kinds of things. Think of me as … I don't know. A spy. That's probably the best description though … not entirely accurate … can we talk about this when I'm not worrying about being shot at?"

"If you tell me who might shoot us, yes."

"The Tol'An. Haven't you heard about them? The jack asses that attacked us before? They're doing it again and this time, it looks like they want to do something that might well destroy the entire planet. Believe me, we do *not* want them to get inside and get to their objective. It'll be way worse than you can even imagine."

"I don't know about that," Tammy grunted. "They really want this bad! What have we done to them?"

"It's what everyone's done I'm afraid." Cassie paused and checked their coordinates. They were getting close to the open door. "The Tol'An believe they know better about how to run the galaxy. They're pushing hard to be the ones in charge. We're pushing back ... with our allies, we're making sure they don't pretty much destroy society."

"They would do that? I thought they were terrorists. That's how the news described them at least."

"That's the best way to say it but they're zealots. They firmly believe in the righteousness of their cause. They see the way that everyone lives and think they know better. Unfortunately, it takes them to extremes. They'll commit suicide to forward their faith ... and I suspect that's what their plan is today."

"You think they're here to die?"

"If they have to ... those that are here." Cassie hummed. "I wonder how they think they'll take out the Pahxin if they lose so much here ... that's an interesting question." She snapped her fingers. "If they had the help from that militia, they probably figure they'd have what it takes to repopulate their ranks. Wow. To think they might use humans in their military."

"That sounds bad." Tammy shushed suddenly. "Did you hear something?"

Cassie hadn't. *If you'd shut up, I might've*. She kept the thought to herself but it was hard. "Sh." She held up her hand, slowing to a walk. They were in one of the normal corridors, metal walls and floor flashing red under the flashing lights. Just a hundred feet away, they needed to turn right to get to the door.

Footsteps made Cassie stiffen. Two sets. She pressed Tammy against the wall, aiming her weapon. A man emerged, holding an assault rifle. It took her only half a second to realize he was dressed in the Tol'An black uniform. He turned in her direction just as she aimed her weapon, depressing the trigger.

Three rounds popped from her weapon, echoing off the walls and ceiling. Cassie's ears started ringing, Tammy screamed. The Tol'An fell to the ground, blood pumping from his chest and throat for only a few moments before he died. "Wait here!" She shouted the words, charging to the body.

Someone cried out in surprise around the way, speaking the Pahxin language. Cassie hadn't picked up enough to understand his words, especially considering how quickly he was speaking. She lowered herself into a crouch, drawing a quick breath before risking a glance around the corner.

Three more Tol'An approached, moving cautiously. Cassie drew back just as they started firing, lighting the area up with beam weapons. "Run!" She shouted at Tammy, charging down. She had to grab her sister as she ran by, the woman stood paralyzed. She clomped after her until they rounded a corner. Cassie stopped.

"What're we doing?" Tammy shouted. "We have to go!"

"Sh!" Cassie waved her hand at her, then aimed her weapon down the hall. The Tol'An came, running after them at a full sprint. She unloaded her magazine, spraying the weapon to lay down the maximum amount of fire in the smaller area. At least one of them took several shots to the chest and body.

Beams blasted down the hall, their unnerving hum competing with pain filled screams. Cassie checked for an alternative route to the door but they would be going in the opposite direction if they fled. Cassie waited for the fire to die down and leaned out again, shooting back. Two of their pursuers were on the ground.

The third remained standing by leaning on the wall. She caught him in the shoulder and dropped him to the floor. All three writhed about.

"You should wait here," Cassie said. "I'm going to make sure they're dead ... and get one of their weapons."

"Okay ... is that a good idea?" Tammy asked. "And what do you mean make sure they're dead?"

"You don't want to know. Stay here!" Cassie ran out before her sister could ask any more questions, hurrying over to the nearest one. She kept her weapon trained on them, kicking the gun away from the man's hand. Checking them over, she found they had small tablets and weapons. "This all it takes to attack us, huh?"

The man muttered something in Pahxin and spat blood on the floor. One of the others expired. She picked up the beam weapon and checked it over. It was one of the standard Pahxin weapons, something she'd become passably familiar with. Aiming it at the man on the ground, she pulled the trigger.

The beam lanced out and fried him in the chest, ending him in a second. "Guess it works." The final man collapsed unconscious. Cassie sighed, considering him for several moments. She already didn't like the fact she'd just executed a dying man but the other ... he was unconscious.

I can't leave him here to shoot someone else who comes along. Cassie grunted before shooting the man. "Tammy!" She called. "Let's go. These guys are gone." She checked her tablet, noting that they should be able to make up the time fast enough if they hurried. Had the Captain and Vincent made it to the Gnosis? How were they doing?

The thought distracted her only for a moment. Tammy hadn't come out. "God damn it," Cassie muttered. "Tammy! We have to go!"

A man stepped out, dragging Tammy with him. Cassie immediately aimed the energy weapon at him as he pressed a pistol to her sister's head. His black uniform was covered in soot and dust. Blood smeared his cheeks and he looked all around as if he expected to be jumped at any moment.

He shouted something in Pahxin, but Cassie had no idea what he was saying. She thought to turn on her tablet for it. If she did, would he think she was doing something? Would he shoot Tammy?

"Cassie!" Tammy shouted. "Help!"

"Working on it, Tam." Cassie drew a deep breath and let it out. "Can you speak our language? I'd like to talk. Let's figure something out, okay?"

The man glared, his dark eyes wide. It dawned on Cassie he might be afraid. With his buddies dead, he probably had no idea what to do. *Great, we happened upon the first Tol'An that doesn't want to die and now he's taken a hostage.* She slowly waved her free hand in a downward motion. "Just let her go."

He shouted something else, pressing the gun harder against Tammy's head.

I have a shot, Cassie thought. *Am I good enough to take this?*

One mistake and she'd kill her sister, end her life right there but this gun didn't have recoil to contend with. It wouldn't move at all when she fired. Maybe if she could get Tammy to move to the left a little, just enough to provide a better target. He didn't understand their language after all.

"Tammy, press your head against that gun tighter," Cassie said. "Press hard and move at least two inches."

"What are you talking about? That's crazy!"

"I'm not asking you," Cassie replied. "Do it now of you'll probably die."

"Damn it!" Tammy gritted her teeth as she pressed against the weapon, tears streaking her cheeks. She closed her eyes tightly, her whole body going tense. The Tol'An directed his attention down for a brief moment. Cassie fired, putting a beam right dead center of the bridge of his nose.

His body just turned off. No jerking motion, no parting shot. He just dropped to the ground but he dragged Tammy with him. She began to scream like a banshee, freaking out as she struggled to get free of him. Cassie rushed over and dragged her off, pulling her well away from him.

"Are you okay?" Cassie asked.

Tammy punched her on the arm. "What the hell was that? Press harder against the gun? Are you nuts?"

"Did I not just save your life?" Cassie scowled. "Come on! This is a tense situation! I didn't ask you to come here but I'll be damned if you don't get out!" She sighed, checking to be sure they weren't about to be ambushed again. "Be calm, okay? Believe me, neither of us has time for panic."

Tammy wiped her face, bending at the waist. She paced a little and finally nodded, looking her sister in the eyes. "Alright, let's do this. Whatever it is we're doing. I'm sorry … about losing my shit there. This is not my life … I've never seen anything this horrible. Never. And I hope I never do again. But if it's just for now, I'll keep it together."

"Thank you." Cassie patted her shoulder. "I don't mean to be rough on you. Let's go. I hope those were the only guys we'll encounter but God knows there might be more running around. In fact …" They got moving and she contacted Christina. "Hey, I think I lost you for a bit. Are you there?"

"I'm nearly to the Orbs," Christina said. "How about you?"

"We ran into trouble. Five Tol'An were in the base. I had to kill them." Cassie checked her tablet again. "We're just about to the door."

"Okay. Hopefully, there's nothing going on down here. If that's the case, then I'll hang out until this is over but if there is … well, I could use some help probably."

"I'll drop Tammy off at the control room and join you as soon as possible. Cassie out." She glanced back at her sister. "It'll be over soon. At least the exciting part. I'm not sure how much better sitting it out will be but at least you won't have to worry about anyone coming in and shooting you."

"How is it that they can blow up the world from this place?" Tammy asked. "What aren't you telling me?"

"A lot," Cassie replied. "And it's going to stay that way for now. Don't worry. You'll probably figure it all out soon enough. For now … just stay close. I don't want you to get grabbed again."

***

Chapter 7

Ulian arrived on the bridge of the Stalwart, stumbling as the ship shook violently. He took his seat beside Morala, glaring at the view screen. They were engaged with four destroyers and a battleship. On their side, six destroyers were going toe to toe with the smaller ships but they all had plenty of guns to go around.

"Report," Ulian said. "How're we doing?"

"We've engaged their flagship," Morala said. "Torqua's ship took heavy damage. They've limped to the back of our lines but they might have to abandon ship. Our shields are steady at seventy-percent. After taking down two of their destroyers, I went for their throat. I believe Trall's on that ship."

"Viran, hail them." Ulian gripped the armrests on his seat, settling in. He'd run to the bridge and only just caught his breath. "I'd like to try to appeal to Trall's sane side ... if he even has one anymore." He shook his head. "I hope they tortured him into joining them because the thought of him doing so without coercion makes me sick to my stomach."

Morala shook her head. "Begging your pardon, sir, but we should be sending this idiot to the afterlife. There's no reason to parlay with them."

"I have Commander Trall, sir," Viran said.

"You never know, Morala." Ulian turned to Viran. "Put him on the screen." The younger Pahxin appeared a moment later, eyes set in a scowl. He wore his hair short and maintained a gaudier form of the Tol'An uniform. His old honors remained on the chest, badges from the various battles he'd fought. "It's been a long time."

"What do you want, Ulian? You and your friends can't stop us from finishing our mission."

"And what is your mission? Cause chaos?"

"If that's why you contacted me, then I think we need to get back to the fight."

"I want you to surrender," Ulian said. "I want you to come back to your people and stand trial for the crimes you've committed but I can make that easier on you if you help us with whoever is in charge of this ridiculous movement. Tell us where to find him, have all your men stand down, and I swear to you on my honor I'll make this right."

Trall laughed. "In our moment of triumph, you want me to give up? To throw away *my* honor?"

Morala stood. "You threw that away when you joined these scum!" She pointed at the screen. "We're giving you a chance you do *not* deserve!"

"Morala …" Ulian spoke her name in a firm tone. "She's not incorrect, Trall. The passion may not be what I'd convey but you *have* put yourself in this position. They're not honorable, attacking innocent people. And you know full well that you're trying to destroy an entire planet here of innocent people. Be sensible."

"How's this for sense," Trall said. The line went dead and a moment later, the ship shook. Ulian sighed.

"My apologies, sir," Morala said. "I … did not mean to speak out like that."

"It's alright," Ulian replied. "Don't think I didn't feel it too. I thought we could talk him down but even without your outburst, he set his mind to this a long time ago. Erda, focus all attacks on Trall's ship and fire at will. Burn it down."

"Yes, sir." The weapons engaged, the first barrage blasted out and tore into Trall's shields. Ulian prepared himself for a brutal fight. Until their other destroyers could break away and help, two battleships could take shots for a while. *Here we go, folks. Time to see who's still standing at the end.*

***

Gunnery Sergeant Geoff Heathrow found himself on guard duty by the Orbs, standing with several of his fellow marines. They'd been on leave, getting some much-needed downtime when they were ordered to the armory at once. When they arrived and found their power armor waiting for them, he wondered if they knew they'd be needed all along.

Then to be relegated to remaining stationary, away from the action, Heat found that particularly annoying. At least they wouldn't have too many troubles maintaining the perimeter. He and the other six guys, each a veteran of several ops, would likely be able to hold off all but the most overwhelming force.

It took nearly twenty minutes before someone reported to them that they were facing the Tol'An. After that, he had a lot more confidence. He'd fought them plenty of times. The zealots came with numbers, but rarely skill. Their gear was decent. It packed a punch but he didn't worry about them. Not like he had during their first encounters.

Ironic that we were down here before, fighting them off. Heat shook his head. *Everything comes full circle except tomorrow, we'll be heading to* their *home territory, their base. Bastards deserve a real ass kicking for all the trouble they've been causing.*

"Incoming!" Sergeant Alex Gillet called. "I've got someone coming up on us!"

"Relax!" Christina Dawson shouted. "It's just me! I'm here to check in with the techs and you guys." She looked around. "I see no one's gotten this far yet."

"How does she know?" Private Kelly asked.

"No bodies," Private Erskin replied.

"Stow it," Corporate Earnest Vine spoke up.

"We've got this," Heat replied to Christina. "The techs are locked in and we've put a marine in there just in case. Whatever they're planning, they picked the wrong day to pull it off."

"Good." Christina rubbed her chin. "Hm. Let me in. I'll back your guy up until this is over."

Heat shrugged and tapped the panel, opening the door. Christina entered and he locked it again. He had two men positioned down the hall and two on the opposite side. Anyone who made it that far had a lot of hell to get through before they could cause any real damage.

Even then, they'd have a lot of angry technicians, one marine and a special agent all ready to blast them. If they were indeed coming down to detonate the Orbs, Heat felt confident they wouldn't get very far.

Explosions outside kept him on his toes, making him wish they could be out there helping their fellow marines. Heat watched the scanners, listened to the com chatter as they talked about hordes of soldiers charging the walls, ships exploding overhead from anti-aircraft munitions. It was crazy … but it could've been worse.

Captain Kent and his team wiped out the militia that had attacked Gamma Alpha before. That mission probably prevented another hundred soldiers from showing up with equipment to support them. Of course, they would've had more defenders but there was no telling whether or not that would've been enough to hold back such a force.

"Heat," Gillet called out. "I just heard from Agent Alexander. She's securing one of the outer doors, heading up to control."

Heat nodded. "Good. That'll prevent one more attack from coming this way." He checked the scans again. "I think we're good though. Most of the fighting's taking place up in the courtyard." *Which sucks for those guys. I guess we all have our duties but we're better suited for that fight, not sitting on our sorry asses down here.*

A couple gunshots exploded down the hall, the pops loud enough to be less than two hundred feet away. Heat exchanged a glance with Gillet. Their two men nearest the sounds advanced to check it out. Scans indicated people out there, five or six. Friend or foe wasn't painting them properly. He had no idea what to expect.

Surely, the Tol'An didn't make it all the way down here. Heat couldn't believe it. How could they possibly breakthrough? How many troops did they send? He got on the com, trying to connect to Cassie. He figured she might have some idea of what was happening out there, maybe got her fingers on the pulse while making her way toward them.

"Agent Alexander." She sounded winded when she answered.

"It's Heat. How close are you to being down here with the Orbs?"

"I'm just getting to the command center. What's up? Do you need me to hurry?"

"No, I was hoping you knew who was standing at our door." Heat paused as his men disappeared around a corner. "We heard gunshots. Trying to determine who's about to pay us a visit."

"It's not me. Did Christina make it?"

"Yeah, she's inside. If you can find a way to be more useful up there then do it. We're stacked up down here." Heat looked at Gillet, motioning down the hall with his head. The man headed off to check on the others. "We'll keep hold down here. Check in with the Gnosis. I'm curious about what's happening there."

"Will do," Cassie said. "Talk to you soon."

The line went dead. A barrage of gunfire erupted down the way. Heat didn't hesitate, charging toward the action with his weapon leading the way. He came upon Gillet firing down the hall before ducking back into cover. One of the marines was down, lying flat on this back and another unarmored man had been half melted.

"What the hell?" Heat asked. "How many?"

"Six," Gillet replied. "Down from eight."

"That Private Pring?" Heat gestured to the downed marine in armor. Gillet nodded.

"He's still alive. Unconscious … injured … but if we get him medical aid soon, I think he'll be okay. They're using some pretty nasty energy weapons. Wish we would've brought ours. These older rifles are kind of sad compared to what we've gotten used to." Beams interrupted him, slapping the wall. "What're they trying to do, suppress us?"

"There are two ways in this area," Heat said. "They might be trying to distract us." He got back on the com. "Gillet and I are holding these guys down here. Keep your eyes open for anyone trying to come in from behind. Good chance they're attempting to flank us." He pointed at the hall with his weapon. "My turn to try?"

"Yeah, be my guest," Gillet said. "I already took care of two of them. I think you should deal with the rest."

"You're so dedicated to your job." Heat popped out and fired immediately, not bothering to aim. The enemies hit the ground but not before one of them caught a bullet to the forehead. He dropped backward, dead in an instant. His companions opened up like they were a firing squad, loading the wall up as Heat withdrew to cover. "Jesus!"

"They're dedicated," Gillet said. "I say we let them come to us. We can do what they just did too. They know we can't use our heavier weapons. No rockets and stuff. Or maybe they're just maniacs who are willing to charge us because they figure one way or another, each of them is going to die today."

"Chilling." Heat turned to their downed marine, dropping low. He reached out swiftly, grabbing the man's arm and dragging him back to safety. More energy beams lanced out, striking the floor all around the downed man, nearly taking Heat's arm off in the prospect. "Sons of bitches! Seriously? Light those bastards up, Gillet!"

Gillet poked his weapon around the corner and opened fire without risking a look himself. His weapon barked, shell casings battering the wall before bouncing away on the ground. He aimed the weapon up and down, veering left and right as he rattled until he was empty.

The spent magazine hit the floor with a hollow clatter and he slammed another one home. Heat checked the scans. Five men remained alive and they were stationary. He was about to say something when one of the others from the other side interrupted. "Contact!" Guns went off in that direction as well.

Just then the five men charged, racing forward. Heat continued dragging the marine back toward the Orb room. Gillet moved backward, aiming his weapon to give them some cover. The others reported multiple contacts of at least ten people in the area. The fighting got thick as the hum of beam weapons competed with the rapid pops from high powered rifles.

The first of the terrorists darted around the corner. Gillet practically tore him in half with a quick burst from the left side to the right, just above the waist. The others followed without hesitation, leading with their beam weapons. Heat hit the deck, firing back. Gillet slammed against the wall as one hit his shoulder but he didn't go down.

The firefight lasted less than eight seconds before all the Tol'An lay in pools of blood. Gillet's armor was scorched in the leg, the shoulder and the side where he'd been grazed. The armor on Heat's calf was hot but the padding between his skin and the surface protected him from severe burns.

"Report!" He shouted. "What's going on?"

"We've got wounded," someone shouted but they were so passionate it was hard to tell which man said it. "They don't give a shit if we shoot them!"

"Damn it!" Heat got to his feet. "Can you help, Gillet?" He didn't wait for an answer, rushing back for the carnage. "Scratch that question. Stay there and guard that passage. If any more come that way, I don't want them flanking us. You're on that duty."

"Got it," Gillet said. "Don't think I really wanted to run just now anyway."

"You'd better not be that hurt!" Heat called back. He hurried on toward the crowd of marines. They took turns popping out of cover and firing two at a time, one crouching, one standing. Heat's scan showed they were facing more than fifteen men still with God knows how many bodies on the ground.

How the hell did so many of them get down here? Heat got on the com to control. They were being jammed. *This is incredible!* "Gillet!" He shouted. "We can't talk to anyone down here!"

"Yeah, loud voices are the only way to go right now!" Gillet called back. "What do you want to do?"

"Let's just finish this." Heat looked at the men he was standing with. "They're not going to stop and this one-off shooting isn't going to help." He directed them back toward the door. "Form a fire line over there. As they come out, blow them away. That's the way to take care of this. I want two lines, front-line crouches, the other just above them."

The marines fell back, forming the line. Heat got behind them, finding a decent firing solution to help. His scans showed the Tol'An were nearly on them. "Steady!" He shouted. "They're just about here!"

Two terrorists bolted around the corner. They were cut down before they could even see what they were facing. The others charged in as well, each one acting like they were in some kind Civil war reenactment complete with screaming. If they truly wanted to make their destination, if they were hopeful for completing their objective, they sure didn't prove it.

A couple still got in a couple lucky shots before dying. Two of their front-line marines caught some energy beams, one to the head and another to the body. They went down, a death and severe injury but after a good half minute of constant firing, the Tol'An stopped coming. They finished them off.

The jamming of coms lifted as well.

"That was insane!" Heat got on the com. "Command, this is Heat. I'm down here at the Orbs and we just took out probably twenty Tol'An who charged us. What's the status?"

"Ground troops are contained up top," one of the men said. "We don't read any enemies within the base."

Heat groaned. "That's because we just killed them all! At least the ones we knew about. You'd better be on high alert!"

"Affirmative. We've got this."

"Uh huh." Heat shook his head. "Get the wounded over there. I'll call in a medical team. I can't believe they got this close! Stay vigilant, guys. If they try again, we have to be ready."

***

Desmond and Vincent disembarked their fighters and rushed to the bridge. When they arrived, Zach practically cheered. He relieved Deacon from the pilot's chair and took his place. They were not currently engaged in a firefight but there was plenty of action all around them. Salina put a tactical map up for them to see.

"The mainstay of the fighting has been kept away from orbit here." Salina drew a circle around a section of space. "That's where the majority of the large-scale battle is taking place. Our fighters have joined the Pahxin at these other locations. They're winning through attrition but we've taken some losses."

"How bad?" Desmond asked.

"Casualty reports aren't accurate yet but I've heard some ejections over the com." Salina paused. "Um … we have a problem."

"What's up?" Desmond squinted at the screen but didn't see what she was talking about.

"It appears one of the enemy destroyers …" Salina stood. "It's charging Earth. It's on a collision course."

"You have to be kidding!" Vincent slapped his leg. "We have to stop that thing at all costs."

"Are there any other ships engaged with it?" Desmond asked.

"Negative, it broke away from the others."

"Get after it, Zach. Full speed, weapons hot." Desmond scowled. "That's definitely one way to win the fight. Crash into Gamma Alpha."

"Their own people are down there!" Vincent clenched both his fists. "That's ridiculous! It's insane!"

"It's exactly the kind of thing these pricks do." Desmond checked his screen, noting they would be on the target in less than three minutes. "Time for it to hit orbit?"

"Six minutes," Salina said.

"Christ, we're cutting this close. Zach, can we do enough damage to stop this thing?"

"I think so, sir. Their shields are weak. Likely, they took damage in the fighting and decided they were going down anyway."

"Might as well use the hulk for something useful." Desmond shook his head. "That makes a sick kind of sense."

They went silent on the bridge, watching the screen as the destroyer continued its plunge toward Earth. Battles raged outside, but the only thing Desmond could think about was catching that Tol'An vessel before it made orbit. If they were lucky, if they got there in time, they could prevent a disaster.

And if not … they might be homeless.

God, all those people. Some of our crew. Desmond drew a deep breath, casting aside his fears and focusing on the task at hand. They were almost on them. "Target their reactor. Light them up. Maybe we can have their own systems do some of the work for us. Especially if their shields are low."

Zach tapped his terminal, nodding that he was ready. Deacon took the scan station normally occupied by Cassie. "Sir, I'm picking up a lot of com traffic from our allies … other Earth ships. They're asking about that destroyer, seeing if anyone's got it."

"Let them know what we're doing." Desmond turned to Vincent. "We've got this."

Vincent merely nodded. He stared so intently on the screen, Desmond could practically feel him willing them to go faster. The notion seemed ridiculous but he'd be lying if he said he wasn't trying as well. They might end up with seconds to save the base, possibly the planet if the Orbs went up at the same time.

"In firing range," Zach announced. Desmond's heart pounded in his chest. "Opening fire."

The Gnosis weapons let loose, plowing into the destroyer. They didn't stop, didn't slow down. Much as Desmond hoped for supreme luck, he knew better. It would take more than a single pass to take down something so large. "Damage report," he said just loud enough to be heard.

"Severe," Salina said. "We've torn through their armor. Hull breach in the back. We need to hit them harder if we want to detonate before they enter atmosphere though."

"Hit them again," Desmond said. "And if it doesn't work, initiate ramming speed."

Zach glanced back but didn't say anything. No one did. They knew the stakes and though it likely meant suicide, the planet came first. Even offering that decision made Desmond sick. He just decided for every soul on board that they would essentially have to die. *But what are the lives of us few for all?*

"Firing again." Zach launched another series of blasts. Everything went at them, hammering the destroyer. The front of the enemy ship began to smoke, catching fire from touching the upper atmosphere. "Direct hits all around!"

Desmond sighed. "We're too late! It didn't—"

Before he could finish the sentence, the destroyer exploded, bursting in all directions. Streaks of metal entered the Earth's atmosphere, bursting into flames like shooting stars. Zach tapped his controls, slowing them down and veering off but the screen stayed on the glorious visual of that attack vessel disintegrating.

"The reactor went up," Salina said. "As we hoped."

"Yes!" Deacon shouted. He and Zach hooted. Desmond exchanged a look with Vincent, feeling like he'd just run thirty miles.

"Close enough for you?"

"Way too close." Vincent shook his head. "We should join the Stalwart. Try to wrap this up."

"I agree." Desmond turned back to the screen. "Zach, put us on intercept with the Stalwart and get us there in a hurry."

"Yes, sir."

"Maybe we can wrap this up so we can meet the enemy on *their* turf."

***

Ulian winced as the ship shook again, another direct blow from Trall's ship. Their damage report showed minimal but the exchange wouldn't be so benevolent for much longer. He checked his screen to see if the other ships had cleared up their fights yet, the various destroyers in the midst of their action but they were still occupied.

Larger fighters kept harassing them, but the smaller ships wouldn't come near the battlecruiser for fear of being taken out by automated defenses. So they kept the smaller ships from helping. If even two of them could come to their aid, they'd likely make short work of Trall but without them, they exchanged broadsides as the humans said.

"Report from the ground," Morala said. "Our troops helped quell the fighting on the surface. The Tol'An forces have been defeated."

"That's good news." Urial frowned. "I wish that meant I could convince this maniac to surrender."

"I'm picking up a message," Viran said. "From the Gnosis!"

"Put it on screen."

Captain Bradford appeared. "Hey there, Ulian. How's it going?"

"I had quite the ride to get up here and now we're in a punching match. How about you?"

"We had our own excitement but we're on our way to you right now. Shouldn't be long now. Can you use the help?"

"To tip the odds, yes." Ulian checked his screen. "Can you take them on their starboard side? We've hit them there a couple times and they've been redirecting to avoid us."

"No problem. We'll pound them just as soon as we're in range. Bradford out."

Ulian smiled at Morala. "Seems fate is on our side after all. That should be more than sufficient to finish this bastard off. Then, it's just a matter of mopping up."

"Do we have coordinates for the Tol'An base?" Morala asked.

"Yes, we were about to discuss the attack when this happened."

"I recommend we plot the course and head there as soon as this rabble is defeated." Morala lifted her hand. "Hear me out. They will not have time to prepare for us and have no idea whether they were successful or not. The longer we delay getting there, the better chance they have of digging in."

"Still rash." The ship shook again. Ulian grunted. "We'll worry about that after we've survived this conflict. Viran, where is the Gnosis?"

"Coming into range right now," Viran replied. "They're opening fire on the starboard side!"

"Sir," Morala said, "three destroyers have finished their targets and are joining in." Ulian stood, watching as Trall's ship took a swath of fire from multiple sources. The Stalwart joined in, tearing into the target with everything they had. Pieces flew off. The ship turned, trying to flee the battle.

"You can't get away, Trall." Ulian sighed. "Trying to flee after talking about honor … sacrificing all those men for no reason. This is disgusting."

"What did you expect from a coward and a traitor?"

"Self-destruct!" Viran shouted. "He's set his reactor to overload!"

"Fool …" Ulian shook his head. "Pull us back, Erda. Give that coward some room to die. Pull back all ships. I don't want anyone caught up in that parting shot." He wanted to spit on the floor. "You disgust me, Trall. I thought you were better than this … than all of this. Instead, you throw it all away for nothing."

Viran gasped. "Sir! I was wrong! No!"

"What?" Ulian spun. "What do you mean?"

"That's not a reactor overload! He just flooded the area with sensor interference. That made it look like that. He's initiated his hyperspace drive!"

"That damaged?" Morala scoffed. "That fool will kill himself!"

"Possibly," Ulian said, "but at least we know where he's going." The ship winked out, escaping the system. "We'll meet up with you soon enough, coward." He turned to Viran. "Order all ships to initiate mop up duties. If any of the Tol'An wish to surrender, accept but ensure they aren't lying. I want all of this cleaned up ASAP. We've got somewhere to be."

Chapter 8

Cassie sat in the shuttle, waiting to board the Gnosis. Gil still hadn't woken up from his coma. She felt lucky but alone with her thoughts, she also worried about ever having to do it again. Especially the next time when all the Orbs would likely be together. That prospect terrified her beyond belief.

Tammy remained in Gamma Alpha, staying in the shelter as the remaining Tol'An forces were rounded up or killed. Many of the smaller ships that still survived were too damaged to flee but continued to cause trouble as they fled toward the moon. Pahxin vessels chased them down to contend with them.

The Stalwart and Gnosis were being dispatched to the Tol'An base, a forward attack force before the rest of the Pahxin fleet arrived from their homeworld. Apparently, more than a hundred ships would arrive inside of six hours. The trip from Earth promised to only take two hours after their navigators worked together.

Intelligence suggested they would be dealing with a minimal force considering what just hit Earth. She wondered if they would encounter any ships at all besides Trall's damaged vessel. He limped away, tail between his legs. Would he even return home? Considering the cost of failure, she almost doubted it.

Then again, he had a twisted sense of honor, one which forced him to face the music. It all depended on how fickle he was feeling in her opinion. After all, if he could pick and choose what mattered to him, why wouldn't he put his life first over all other things? The greatest honor to cowards was remaining alive for one more day.

The shuttle landed at the same time as another one. When she disembarked, Heat and his team were as well. They were all the last people to have to board the ship before it departed for Tol'An space. She waved to him, offering a smile. He nodded, looking grim. She'd heard he lost a couple men during the fight.

Those marines have taken a serious beating since we started all this. Cassie headed out, head bowed. *I hope we find a way to make it up to the survivors.*

"Cassie!" Vincent shouted from down the hall. He rushed over to her, pulling her into a hug. "God, I'm glad to see you! Are you okay?"

Cassie nodded. "I'm fine."

"You sure? Nothing going on up in the head?"

"Running around seemed to cure me," Cassie replied. "Anyway, how're you? I heard you had to fly yourself up?"

"In a fighter. It was a little wild. You ready for this?"

"Yeah. I can't wait for it to be done."

"Me either." Vincent gestured with his head. "Shall we head to the bridge? We're about to initiate hyperspace now that you're all aboard."

"That's where I was heading. Did you guys hear about who we lost on the marine front?"

"A couple more ..." Vincent frowned. "Energy weapons. Lucky shots on our power armor can kill a man quick. Anyway, I don't have specifics. They've been logged in the report. I just haven't had time to go over it yet. We had the fastest war council I've ever seen, all done remotely with the different commanders on their various ships."

"Probably what we needed to do in the first place."

"How was your sister?" Vincent asked. "I never had the chance to ask how your meeting went then she ended up getting in the middle of this mess."

"She showed up to cut me out of her life," Cassie said. "I'm sure she's all the more determined to do that now after what happened. But at least she's safe. She's remaining in Gamma Alpha until we get back. I guess she wants to hear how the story ends since she got caught up in the final chapters."

"I'm curious myself." Vincent hit the elevator button and they boarded. "We have no idea what to expect when we get there. Could be next to nothing left. There's so much debris around Earth right now, they estimated we'll be salvaging junk and parts for over a year. Can you even imagine that?"

"And that's all the stuff that didn't burn up in the atmosphere." Cassie turned to him. "Did you hear some of those larger pieces of the destroyer went down in the sea? They're being picked up by some navy or other. I guess it was big enough to send the water up more than two hundred feet into the air … though maybe the report exaggerated."

"Yeah, big chunks and some think that they'll be useful … like computer parts. I doubt it." Vincent rubbed his eyes. "That was one of the scariest chases I've ever experienced in my life. We knew what would happen if we didn't stop them … and only barely did. If they weren't already damaged, that could've been bad."

"You saved us all." Cassie took his hand and squeezed it. "Thank you."

"I would have to give all the credit to Zach, to be honest." The doors opened, interrupting more conversation. "We'll talk later, huh?"

"Of course." Cassie took her seat. "Good morning everyone. You'd think we'd get a rest after everything that happened, huh?"

Salina chuckled.

"At least we get two hours of downtime," Desmond said. "Welcome back, Cassie. I'm glad you're here. This is it, folks. Now that you're all here and we're about to drop into hyperspace, I think it's time to address the crew. Salina, put me on ship wide speakers. I've got a little something prepared."

Cassie leaned back in her seat as the connection was established, watching Desmond curiously.

"Crew of the Gnosis. Not long back, we were testing this vessel's faster than light capability. We jumped out to Pluto and were on the verge of conducted some further tests when our planet was attacked. Most of you were there with us that day, experiencing the dread of rushing back. Even that short jump home felt too long given the circumstances.

"When we arrived, we found ourselves faced with an alien foe, one we'd never even imagined. They were not necessarily more advanced but they definitely had an agenda, one which meant the theft of the very object that put us in space. We resisted them then and conducted a secondary mission, preventing them from acquiring a second device.

"That started the war with the Tol'An. They came to our home, our planet and assaulted us. We responded in defense but soon found ourselves wrapped up in a conflict far more involved than a mere terrorist organization harassing a small planet in the Sol system. No, we found ourselves engaged with a zealous enemy intent on conquering known society.

"They want to run the lives of their brothers, the Pahxin. We're just a thing that's in the way, a thorn in their sides. We're good at that. Human beings have always stood in the way of bullies and criminals, always found the side of honor to be preferable to villainy. Today, we prove that conviction by taking up arms with our allies.

"Each of you has done a great deal to get here. I'm proud of you. We have all sacrificed so much. Equipment, ships, friends … the lives we've lost in this war will not be forgotten nor will they easily be forgiven. As we drop into hyperspace today, we will be racing toward the conclusion of this wretched organization.

"We will annihilate them and liberate the devices they've hoarded. Our Pahxin allies are even more motivated, having suffered at the hands of the Tol'An for far too long. Those of you who joined me when I came aboard the Gnosis hoped to become explorers. I'm here to tell you that this final obstacle stands between us and that goal.

"When we're done, we will finally see the stars, unafraid of those who would demand we live *their* way. Never forget, humanity does not back down to threats from scum. We are strong. *You* are strong. We will win the day as we won this conflict over our own planet. Thank you again for your hard work. I appreciate you."

Desmond waved his hand at Salina. She killed the connection. "There you go, folks. My speech for the day."

"Didn't sound too rehearsed," Vincent replied. He grinned. "You did a good job."

"I hope it inspires something other than sarcasm," Desmond said. "Anyway, I firmly believe all of that and those of you on this bridge with me, you've done exceptional work. I could think of no one else I'd rather be flying into battle with today than all of you. Thank you for being here."

Cassie turned to her station, peering at the screen. She also believed in what he said, despite the fact she felt like some sort of skepticism should've kept her from glowing. Christina or Dulain would've scoffed, she thought but the speech gave her hope. The future shouldn't be about wars and secrets. It should be about discovery.

That's what they wanted all along and when this fight ended, they would finally get it.

***

Gizan watched the vast majority of the Tol'An fleet depart the system, tucked safely amongst a cluster of natural debris. He couldn't help but smile as he considered how the opposition dwindled while the chances of his success increased. He would soon see Ezria face to face and conclude his business with the man once and for all.

His former master must've felt particularly safe to allow for so much of his force to depart. They revealed their destination to be Earth, a full-scale attack to destroy the Trindishas there and potentially cripple the human's ability to fight. Some of them were going there to die, sacrificed to the cause but Trall believed in his success.

The man came over the com a few times sounding smug as he gave orders. Gizan wished he would have the opportunity to sink a blade in that man's throat as well. He found him to be a foppish, conflicted buffoon willing to sell out his values and pride at a moment's notice for any reason.

Gizan questioned his own integrity as well but at least he left the Tol'An behind. Trall continued to bootlick, following orders from a total madman in the process. He was primarily motivated by revenge against the military that cast him out, which was a dangerous thing to play with. Ezria should've known better.

Calatha would have. He understood the universe and how best to approach problems. Violence was a final option, not the first. *I'll remind Ezria of this fact when I finish him off ... though I suppose I may not be practicing the philosophy either.* Gizan shook his head. *But then I was not the chosen leader of the Tol'An either.*

Gizan didn't need a clear conscience. He didn't need to feel superior to his target. He merely needed to do away with him to find freedom. If that meant sacrificing integrity, he did not care. The galaxy would be a better place without Ezria in it and when he was gone, then the last traces of the brief philosophical movement could fade.

We started with such positive notions. Help the people live properly. It became corrupted. Power twisted Ezria. He became convinced of his superiority rather than the cause to do away with corruption, debauchery, wickedness. They became the nightmares they hoped to abolish. Instead of paving the way for a peaceful society, they became criminals.

Murderers really. Calatha told Gizan that he would have to get his hands dirty, that he would be the blade in the night. That was acceptable given the goal, the end result but he never anticipated how far it would go. Converting people against their will. Conscripting individuals. Killing those who refused.

That was not the goal of the Tol'An, not originally.

"I'm ready to approach," Rythi interrupted his thoughts. "It'll take several hours but it's going to be even easier now with all those ships gone. Their scans seemed to be pretty decent but I've got ways around them. So ... I guess what I'm saying is if you're ready to go, I'm ready to get you there."

"By all means, captain." Gizan patted the man on the shoulder. "Bring us in. I'd like you to bring up a topographical map for me so I can show you specifically where I'd like to land. Can we do that or are we bound to something specific to remain out of sight?"

"Well, we can't land in their hangar," Rythi said, "but other than that, we have few limitations. Visual is still a problem. My recommendation is we approach from the far side of the planet, drop low and fly close to where you want. We'll be under scans, out of sight and put down without anyone knowing we even entered the atmosphere."

"Indeed. You do know what you're doing. I'm good with this approach."

Rythi engaged the engines. "We basically do this with controlled, randomized bursts, maintaining a consistent speed. If for some reason they do find us, they'll think we're junk. Have you noticed the theme? Always look like debris. Everyone ignores trash, even when they shouldn't."

"Yes, I wish I would've known this before ... or at least understood it to the degree you do. In fact, you seem like the kind of man I needed on many jobs. A shame I was on an even darker side of the law than you are now. It makes for poor companions when you are wanted by every authority."

"I'm halfway there," Rythi said. "At least the Kalrawv Group leaves me alone for the most part."

"Soon, you will be free." Gizan stood. "I'm going to rest before we arrive. Wake me when you're an hour out. I'd like to be here when we're about to make our descent to the planet's surface. One last sleep before meeting my fate ... and hopefully turning the tide for the entire galaxy."

***

Desmond sat in his office, staring up at the ceiling. Their rapid departure had not been how he envisioned the attack on the Tol'An. He anticipated more planning, time to work out the details while they compiled a larger fleet. All the different branches that wanted in on the action, all the military leaders were suddenly silenced in the wake of the attack.

An attack which took place over the planet and on a small section of one of the contents. Most of the world didn't even know about it until the media announced it. One of the Pahxin stated it the best: they needed to act quickly because as soon as the Tol'An leadership realized they'd lost everything, they might scatter to the wind.

If their enemies managed to pack up the Orbs and run off with them, they'd have to track them to a new place. No one had the stomach to let the situation linger any longer than it had to. Admiral Reach was able to use that to his advantage and run with it, ensuring that he had the authority to send the Gnosis with the Stalwart as forward scouts.

No one believed the Tol'An had anything of significance to throw at them. Trall, the coward who ran at the end, might be there when they arrived but he couldn't stand against them both. Not when he barely managed to do so while he still had his defenses up. The worst part of his fleeing involved the fact he would be able to warn his fellow terrorists.

The com drew his attention to the desk. "Captain, it's Vincent. We're about to emerge from hyperspace. Ten minutes."

"I'm on my way." Desmond grabbed his jacket and pulled it on, preparing himself for the final round. He didn't anticipate there'd be anything left by the time the rest of the fleet arrived and he was okay with that. This situation felt personal, like something they needed to accomplish on their own.

Having the Stalwart along made it feel like two companions from some old story, finishing a task long in the making. Desmond couldn't imagine another ship sharing the risk and glory with them. Rocky as they started out, he came to like Ulian and his crew. They were excellent representatives of their culture.

And soon, we'll get to find out how well we all play together when there isn't a threat looming over our heads. God, I hope we have the maturity to make this work. We don't need another conflict ... especially one we could not win.

***

Heat boarded a shuttle for what seemed like the hundredth time. He demanded to go on the final mission, to be the one to help bring the Orbs back to the ship. After everything he'd been through, nothing would've stopped him from getting out there, even if he did feel exhausted. The consistency of their missions was definitely getting to him.

Lieutenant Brent Fielding finally felt up to joining them and he'd be leading the mission. Heat knew the man hated sitting around on the ship waiting for them to get back. Just the way he sounded throughout the operations showed he wanted to be in the thick of things, despite the danger.

Especially when they procured the last Orb and dealt with the strange space station that effected men's minds. Privately, Heat thought the lieutenant should be happy he didn't have to go on that one. It very well might've resulted in his death. Heat thought he'd seen everything before they set foot in that place.

He was wrong.

Come to think of it, I can't believe the things I've dealt with. Mental connectivity to ancient alien relics, meeting a race of people who copied themselves into a computer, that haunted ass space station ... They don't put this shit on a recruitment poster because people would think they were advertising for a movie, not the marines.

"You guys ready?" Fielding asked. The marines they had with them were an odd bunch, mostly comprised of men who had been with them since the beginning. Sergeant Gillet, Corporal Vines, Privates Kelly, and Erskin all made up the real veterans. In addition to them, Lieutenant Brady Dashwood came along and a Corporal Dustin "The Rat" Mink.

The last poor bastard supposedly dealt with the nickname since he attended boot.

The Pahxin planned on backing them up with twenty men total. Those numbers should've been overkill unless intel was grossly misinformed about the Tol'An numbers. Once the dust settled back at Gamma Alpha, they estimated the vast majority of their enemy's resources had been spent.

This trip is more of a coup de grace than an actual brawl.

The marines responded to Fielding with a determined, but quiet *ho-ah*. Only the two new guys seemed truly pumped up but then, they'd never been to space before. Both of them stared out the window until they went into hyperspace and even afterward, they kept carrying on about how incredible it was.

Heat didn't think he ever felt quite so enthusiastic about space but he hadn't heard any stories. These two marines heard the rumors about what they'd seen and done, how many battles they'd been in and all that jazz. Photos of the environments they visited circulated around Gamma Alpha, psyching people up to take to the stars when it was safe.

After so many people died during their missions, Heat couldn't help but feel cold about the prospect of exploration. Yes, they technically found themselves at war, that didn't help him acclimate to those losses any easier. Part of him tried to justify it, talk about how the other soldiers knew what they were getting into but it didn't help.

The names immediately came to his mind. Privates Howards, Taras, Bosh, Wheeler, Dorian, Brock, and Singer ... all gone. Corporal Willis Anderson, a man Heat had worked with prior to joining the Gnosis died in their last mission. They lost Lieutenant Colby Topper during the first time out.

That didn't count the entire team he'd barely met that lost their lives on their prior mission. They all bothered him, all bit right to the soul but the one loss that still got him down was his good friend, Sergeant Lawrence Gorman. He sacrificed himself for the team, saved them all. The heroics didn't make the loss any easier.

Heat always believed he'd remain in the military for life, retire there. As they prepared to hit the Tol'An planet, he realized this was likely his last run. When they finished, he would leave the marines, enter civilian life and try to put it all behind him. But before that happened, before he risked boredom in some crappy part of the world, he needed to finish the fight.

The ship started to shake. Dashwood looked around frantically. "Should we be worried about that? Was that okay? Are we cool?"

"We are," Gillet said. "I don't know what your problem is."

"Screw you, man. This is new to me!"

"We're fine," Fielding replied. "We've just left hyperspace. Depending on how close we are to the planet, this shuttle will launch soon. Considering who helped us with coordinates, I'm thinking we'll be pretty darn close. Should be a neat little run down to the surface, a brief fight into the complex and a hell of a time figuring out how to get the Orbs home."

"Piece of cake, huh?" Heat said. "Sounds like we've got all the bases covered."

"We got it at the mining facility," Fielding pointed out. "And you figured it out in that terrifying space station. I have supreme confidence in us. Besides, if intel's right for a change, we should practically be able to walk into their mostly abandoned base. Show of hands who's betting on that?"

No one moved.

"Yeah, me too." Fielding lifted his finger. "One second, Captain Gabriel's contacting me about our current location."

Heat admired his HUD, ensuring everything was online and ready to go. They were sending three shuttles just in case something happened. Combined with the four heading down from the Pahxin, they were guaranteed to have a ride back for the Orbs. *Yeah, but this is the wrong objective.*

When they left Sol, Heat commented to Fielding that they should be looking for the leader of the Tol'An and taking him out. The Orbs should've been a secondary objective. Command disagreed, stating they were too dangerous to leave in the wild. Even if the Tol'An elite got away, it didn't matter so long as they brought the devices with them home.

If they feel cornered, they might detonate them. Heat wondered if the terrorists knew how to weaponize the Orbs. He somehow doubted it but they had used them to forge some interesting trinkets. The engineering teams had a field day with their gadgets and computer equipment. Nothing too fancy, but it filled in some blanks about the enemy.

"Okay," Fielding said. "We're launching now. Opposition out there is light. We'll have a straight shot to the planet. Four ships escorting us. Now's the time, guys. Get ready to kick some ass!"

Heat's private com went off. He accepted the incoming call, setting his helmet to privacy mode. It masked his voice so that no one could hear it outside of his com. "Hello?" He said while tapping his leg.

"It's Cassie. I wanted to talk to you just before you left."

"Too late," Heat replied. "We're on our way right now."

"I meant before you go to the surface, you maniac. I've got the coordinates of the Orbs. I'm sending them to your whole unit. Looks pretty good for your run. There's a battleship but the captain assures me it was severely damaged before it fled Earth. Three destroyers are also here. They really did commit everything to the attack."

"Bad for them." Heat smirked. "Good for us. Should be a piece of cake. Got any idea how many soldiers we're facing?"

"I'm afraid not. Salina's doing a full system sweep, trying to find anything out of the ordinary. I'll keep you informed as I can. Hey …" Cassie lowered her voice. "Try to be really careful when you get down there, okay? Those Orbs … with two of them right next to each other, you might be impacted by them. They *could* reach out."

"I don't want to end up like Gil," Heat said. "I really need to learn how to ignore these damn things. You know … block them from hopping into my head."

"I'm working on a way," Cassie said, "but it's slow going. Hopefully, Gil's awake when we get back. He might have some ideas. And Thayne's definitely working on it. He and Harper have a bunch of theories but unfortunately, those aren't helping us any. Not you and I, especially."

"How bad was that last contact you had?"

"Bad. I thought it was fifteen minutes and it turned out to be several hours. Those things are no joke and all six of them together ... it makes me *very* nervous."

"Probably not a good idea to have them all in the same room." Heat sighed. "Not my call though. Hey, we're on approach now. I'm going to get off the line ... put my game face on, you know the drill."

"Good luck. We'll be in touch soon."

"Thanks." Heat killed the line and turned to glance out the window. They were on rapid approach to the planet. The Stalwart already jumped the destroyers, laying into them with a shocking display of firepower. Energy blasts battered the smaller ship which tried to maneuver away.

It didn't matter. A moment later, the hull ruptured and it began to list, drifting off as the reactor exploded. Two chunks began to float apart, electric pulses dancing along the damaged sections. Heat shook his head. *Those Pahxin guys are tough. They've got some fantastic weapons. I do* not *look forward to ever having a brawl with them.*

"Six minutes," Fielding shouted. "This is what we trained for, folks! Hold on to something 'cause this might be rough!"

Probably not, Heat thought. *We'll probably barely notice other than some turbulence and a little shaking. Otherwise, this will be a routine mission. We'll get in, we'll leave and even though the results will be felt across the galaxy, we'll think of it like any other mission. In fact, we'll have to be convinced otherwise.*

Strange world we live in. Heat checked his weapon then put his game face on. He was ready.

***

Chapter 9

Gizan and Rythi nearly made it to the planet when Trall's ship returned alone. It was badly damaged, scans indicating system failure throughout the ship and limited defenses. It limped back toward the planet, a slow run that would take them the better part of five hours, plenty of time for the small passenger ship to make its run.

They arrived at the edge of the planet twenty minutes ahead of the larger ship. Maintaining their camouflage meant they couldn't move at full speed but it didn't matter. Gizan knew he'd be in position long before Trall had a chance to report back whatever bad news he carried. Likely that he lost the entire fleet.

Rythi took them into the atmosphere on the far side of the planet where night blanketed the continent. As they plunged toward the surface, the captain didn't engage the thrusters until they were only five thousand feet above the ground. Leveling out, he kept them low, practically skimming trees as they made their way toward the base.

Thirty minutes into the trip, they had almost arrived at their destination. Gizan pumped himself up for what was to come, meditating on what it would take to get into the base to find Ezria. More importantly, he needed to consider the sheer number of men he might face and how he planned to dispatch them all.

Stealth was the only option but he also needed to be quick. It would be a challenge, but he knew he was up to it.

Rythi drew him out of his personal meditation with a sigh and a clicking of his tongue.

"What's the matter?" Gizan asked. "What is it?"

"Two ships just jumped into the sector," Rythi replied. "And they must've had a crack navigator because they're practically right on top of the planet." He hummed. "Do you recognize either of these vessels? One's a Pahxin battleship, that's for sure but I've never seen the other one before. Some kind of experimental craft?"

Gizan looked at the screen and groaned inwardly. "That is a human ship," he muttered. "The Gnosis."

"You know it then. Is it dangerous?"

"Terribly but I shouldn't be surprised that they came right after Trall. That fool. I wonder if he led them back here or if they figured out how to make the Orbs show them where we were. Well, they complicate matters … and make it so I have to move even swifter."

"Can you still do it?" Rythi turned to him. "Gizan, I know that you feel like you've got to do this, but I'd be remiss in saying ... once we got over the whole holding a knife up to me thing, I've come to respect you some. I'd rather not see you throw your life away unnecessarily. Seriously."

"What do you propose?"

"I can get us out of here right now," Rythi gestured to the controls. "We can be out of this system in the next half hour. Let these people kill each other. You don't have to be part of their nonsense anymore. Especially now that the Pahxin have arrived to take care of the Tol'An. What's the point of getting in their way?"

Gizan considered his comments for a long moment. The fact he expressed any sort of companionship shocked him. Perhaps he made a valid point. Once the Tol'An were gone, no one would be pursuing him, not effectively. And all he had to do was tell the captain to pull up, depart the planet.

"How will you get paid?" Gizan asked. "The wealth I promised you is in that base."

"One thing you learn when you take to spacing," Rythi said. "There's always a way to make money."

"Fascinating thought." Gizan rubbed his eyes. "No, we have to finish this. I need to be the one to take care of Ezria and if that means I face the humans again … face Pahxin soldiers, then so be it. If for some reason they capture you, I'll tell them I forced you to come here. You'll be exonerated."

"I won't be caught," Rythi said. "I'm not as comfortable with you getting away."

"It might not be my destiny to escape." Gizan gestured to the screen. "That's where we're landing."

"Yeah …" Rythi brought them in by a grove of trees, setting the ship down with all the finesse of a surgeon. He turned to Gizan. "I wish you luck. Don't do anything foolish. If you don't think you can make it happen, come back. I'm telling you. We can make a life somewhere else for you. It doesn't have to be after you kill someone."

"I do appreciate it." Gizan gripped his shoulder for a moment. "Drop the hatch. I've got a bit of a run ahead of me." The loading ramp dropped, slapping the ground hard. Gizan jogged off the ship and turned sharply, heading for the base he'd spent the majority of the past three years.

This would be the last time he ever saw it. One way or another, he'd never look upon it again.

***

Ulian leaned forward as the Stalwart left hyperspace. The screen flickered on a moment later, revealing three destroyers and Trall's ship, sidling up to an old space station. Records indicated the system hadn't been visited in over a hundred years. Any facilities they utilized were either ancient or put into service by the Tol'An.

None of this looks particularly new. Ulian scowled at their opposition. *Especially those ships. They appear to be military vessels. Probably stolen ships that Trall helped them acquire somehow.* The thought boiled his blood but he maintained his composure, keeping his tone even as he spoke.

"Engage." Ulian leaned back. "Erda, fire at will. I want those destroyers gone. Get a scan of the surface and scramble our shuttles. I want the humans to have all the backup they need. I believe we can make short work of this force and wrap this up prior to the fleet's arrival. Make it happen."

Erda pushed them to full speed, adjusting course to take them directly to their targets. Their coordinates proved solid enough that they closed within firing range within twenty minutes. During that time, the smaller ships moved to meet them, preparing for a fight. Tactical showed them powering up shields and weapons.

They're insane, Ulian thought. *They can't possibly think they can beat us.* He turned to Morala. "If they're willing to throw their lives away at us, it's because they're trying to buy time for something else. Are those shuttles going?"

"Yes, sir," Morala answered. "They're on their way. Humans hopped in right after us and made straight for the planet. They're depositing their marines with air coverage. Soldiers will have boots on the ground within twenty minutes if they hurry as much as I'm sure they will. The Gnosis should be able to join us shortly to finish off Trall."

"We can hold them off until then." Ulian paused as Erda fired the weapons, blasting the first destroyer. The ship veered hard to starboard, an attempt to evade but too many of the blasts struck them center mass. Shields ruptured but it took a second pass of weapons to cut them in half, blowing them into two chunks. "As expected. The other two?"

"They're moving to flank us," Erda said. "I can broadside them both."

"Trall is hailing us," Viran said. "I have him on the line if you'd like to talk to him."

Ulian considered ignoring the man but he ultimately couldn't do it. "Erda, do not let up on those destroyers." He hummed. "I suppose we can hear him snivel. What do you say, Morala?"

"Of course, sir."

"Put him on the screen."

Trall's face appeared, this time wearing a fearful expression. "Ulian …" He swallowed hard after his voice broke. "Sir. You cannot do this. You cannot destroy everything we've worked so hard to build."

"Are you appealing to me to allow known terrorists to flourish?" Ulian asked. "Because if so, I'm inclined to think you have become funny. Though I doubt that could be true considering how you're sweating." He rubbed his chin. "Intriguing that you would even think to contact me with such a complaint."

"How dare you—"

"How dare *you*!" Ulian interrupted with a shout, startling his bridge crew. "You betrayed your people for this! You refused to surrender when given a chance. You've thrown away everything you vowed to protect. I have no time for games or conversation. This is the end for you, Trall. You have two choices: accept it like a man or snivel like a child."

"But we can work something out!"

"I'm done." Ulian waved his hand at Viran who killed the line. The ship trembled from an attack. "The destroyers I take it?"

"Yes, sir. They're hitting us with missiles. Shields are at eighty percent. They'll have a hard time punching through."

"Sir …" Viran sighed. "Trall is … well … it looks like he's going to ram us."

Ulian slapped his forehead. "That fool headed idiot!" He scowled. "How long before he gets here?"

"Five minutes."

"Can we launch bombers in that time, Morala?"

"I can get them up in two … I'm not sure if they'd be effective at taking him down in time. It would be better to use the missile launchers and put the warheads on those. They're not as maneuverable from weight but it shouldn't matter if he's going in a straight line."

"The weapon crews can do it in time?"

"I'll be sure they do." Morala got on the com and started barking orders.

"Viran, inform the Gnosis what this idiot is planning and tell them we need all the firepower they can muster brought to bear." Ulian turned to Erda. "If worse comes to worst, you can get us out of his way, right?"

"It won't be fun for the crew but I can." Erda hummed. "I'm calculating an escape vector right now. It might be close though, considering how little warning we got about it. Can I just say this guy really annoys me, sir?"

"You're mirroring my thoughts." Ulian stood. "Now this comes down to whether or not we can load a gun fast enough to destroy a madman. Down to the alacrity of our people in the hold. This is where we see whether drills pay off or are completely worthless. Training versus desperation. May the best ship win."

***

Vincent confirmed their ships were launched. He was about to inform Desmond when Salina cursed. "Sir," she said, "the Stalwart just reported that the Tol'An battleship is on a collision course with them. Estimated Time to Impact is less than five minutes. They've asked we bring all firepower to bear on that ship."

"Get us over there, Zach," Desmond said. "As fast as you can."

"I'm on it." Zach tapped his controls and the ship started moving, veering to the left. "ETA less than two minutes."

"Lord, this is a close one." Vincent clenched his fist. "What is with these guys and their suicide attacks? Do they not realize dying is not winning?"

"They know their time is done," Desmond replied. "This is how they give up. Not by surrendering to live out their lives in a prison or be executed but going out on their own terms. It's disturbing but that's the zealous mind." He turned to Cassie. "Are our people going to be able to find the Orbs easily enough?"

"I have their coordinates and I sent them to each of the marines," Cassie replied. "They have what they need. Now it's just a matter of dealing with however many enemies are still down there."

"Do we have an accurate count yet?" Desmond asked.

"Negative," Salina said. "The Orbs are interfering with surface scans. I can tell you there are people but not how many. Wait." She cleared her throat. "Cassie, look at this. This interference is coming from outside the base. About a mile away. Do you see that? Some kind of object is causing it."

Vincent watched Cassie take a look. She returned to her seat and tapped at her console. "Size and silhouette suggest a ship," she said. "Do you see?"

"Is it a ship or some kind of jamming beacon they set up?"

"Definitely a ship."

"But it's emitting a signal that makes this appear natural. Clever … but annoying." Salina shrugged. "I don't see how to get around it. It's almost like this thing is compensating for everything I try. Wouldn't you think that would be suspicious? I mean, come on!"

Cassie shrugged. "The casual observer might just think they weren't good enough to get around the natural emanations of the planet. We know what we're doing. I'm not sure it ultimately matters. There can't be enough people down there to make a difference. Not considering how many soldiers are on their way."

"We'll get a scan from the fighters," Vincent said. "I'm sure proximity will play into it." He looked at his screen. "Our shuttles are half way down. Meeting no resistance so far."

"That's what I thought," Desmond replied. "We already took out most of what they have. Zach, are we in firing range?"

"Thirty seconds."

"Push it. They ram the Stalwart and that should be enough to finish the fight there." Desmond leaned forward. "I'd rather not be in the midst of a rescue operation when the rest of the fleet arrives."

***

Gizan moved swiftly through the trees, an environment he'd become intimately familiar with over the past several years. He trained out there alone, running and performing martial arts forms he'd learned in his youth. Few knew just how much time he spent in the wild and fewer still knew all the secrets of the Tol'An as he did.

The inlet to the sea was far to the north. Ezria's personal chambers overlooked it. That's where the man would likely be, lost in a delusion, blinded by the belief that he would survive this final attack. He probably thought some fleet was coming to save him, the remnants of what he sent against Earth.

That was not to be. Gizan saw Trall's ship and it was in shambles. It had taken a pounding and probably shouldn't have even survived the trip back. The fact it did was a miracle but now that the human ship arrived along with their allies, they'd finish what they started back on Earth.

I hope they don't bombard the base before I finish my work. Gizan didn't know how far the Pahxin would go to eliminate the Tol'An threat but he knew how they were considered in the top five largest threats to the government. That was a wise decision when they were clever, but they'd probably been dramatically demoted.

Or maybe not. The Pahxin like to see things through.

The outer doors came into view, the side entrance he often used to exit the base. No one stood guard, as he hoped. Darting from the trees, he made his way to the door and entered the old code. The door slid open. *The fools! They haven't changed the security? Trall should've known better than that even if Ezria did not.*

But who would think that Gizan was coming back? He'd fled, left his responsibilities behind and seemed to be gone. Only the fact that Ezria sent people after him made him decide to strike back and buy his freedom with this last, personal mission. Still, he thought he instilled some honest paranoia in them.

Maybe they have bigger fish to fry. Gizan paused before entering, turning to see shuttles fast approaching. Human and Pahxin soldiers, racing down to collect the Trindishas he assumed. If he wanted to survive, he needed to slip in, perform his deed and get back to Rythi. If the man was as good as he said, he could get them out of there unseen.

Gizan slipped into the base, moving down the familiar corridors. Men shouted up ahead, the remaining defensive force getting into position to hold back the invaders. He wished he had his uniform still. He might've melded amongst them, slipping by unnoticed. As it was, he remained in the shadows, giving them a moment to get outside.

You fools should remain inside, Gizan thought. *Make them come to you. Blast them when they attempt to enter. Instead, you'll be obliterated as soon as they get out of their ships. And that's if they don't bombard the place prior to deploying their soldiers. The Tol'An needed better leaders ... men with experience.*

Gizan watched the staging area where the men poured out of two double doors. All but two charged outside, making their way for defensive positions. Those who lingered displayed something that would've gotten them shot if their commander saw it: fear. They didn't want to risk their lives fighting the enemy outside.

I don't blame you, Gizan thought. *But I have to get by.* The room was large but not so big that they wouldn't notice his passage. He sprinted toward them, both knives drawn. They turned at the last possible second, opening their mouths to cry out. He plunged his weapons into their throats, taking them both to the ground with his momentum.

They flailed, one managing to grab Gizan's wrist before expiring. The others outside had no idea, didn't look back. Two men died from cowardice, a truth which spoke of the decline of the organization as a whole. If they could sense the decline, if their zeal lifted, then the Tol'An were in the midst of similar death throes.

Gizan grabbed one of their weapons and slung it over his shoulder. He dragged them to the side, out of casual view then ran down the hall again. Passing through the operational area, he saw men working through windows into the other rooms. They were organizing the defense efforts but none of them looked around.

Next, he'd enter the living quarters before approaching Ezria's lair.

The walls trembled as the assault commenced. *Those attacks must be hitting the ground. If they were battering the building, it would feel like world ending seismic activity. No, they're hitting those idiot soldiers outside. There must be more in here somewhere. Possibly guarding their master. It will not be enough.*

***

Ulian did his best to maintain his reserve but inside, he seethed. The fact that Trall would conduct himself with such a blatant dishonor came off as reprehensibly desperate. The rogue captain had so many options, even running away would've been better. But instead, he charged, giving up all sense of propriety in the process.

The final two destroyers laid into them, though Ulian wasn't sure why. If Trall was successful, they wouldn't have to bother. They should've turned their attention to the Gnosis, which took position on the enemy's starboard flank. Would they be able to handle the two smaller ships with the Stalwart gone?

"Target's in range," Erda said. "Opening fire."

Their weapons discharged, piercing the hull of the enemy vessel and tearing through their weakened shields. Pieces flew clear but the mainstay of the ship remained intact. They didn't need much for a ram to be effective. If they were able to hit them with reasonable momentum, both vessels would be disabled at best or worst, utterly destroyed.

The Gnosis let loose as well, battering at the enemy with a full barrage. Their attack brought about similar results, ripping panels free and exposing several decks. Ulian calculated the loss of life, how many people aboard were being slaughtered because of Trall's vanity. Regardless of how the situation turned out, all of them would die.

"We're ready with the bombs," Morala announced. "Firing now."

The ordnance streaked away from the ship, leaving behind gray particles. They detonated on impact, cutting large chunks from the vessel. Erda hit the thrusters, carrying them upward fast enough that the artificial gravity and inertial dampeners could not keep up. Ulian grunted from the force as they moved.

He had to do it at the right moment or Trall's people could've adjusted course, maintaining enough momentum to still cause considerable damage. But even with the dramatic maneuver, the enemy battleship attempted to chase them. Flames erupted from seams spread over the craft like throbbing orange veins.

Blow already! Ulian willed their reactor to detonate, to finish them off. He checked his screen. They were less than five thousand kilometers away. Destruction at that range would still cause some damage, the larger pieces in particular. Erda seemed to know that. He hadn't let up on the thrusters.

"Can we fire?" Ulian shouted to fight the pressure making it difficult to breathe. "And why didn't those bombs finish him off?"

"I'm working on it!" Erda said.

"They pretty much worked!" Viran called back. "All their systems are offline. They're basically a projectile heading straight for the planet's surface! They can't maneuver and we're out of their path so can we please slow down now before I vomit? I'd really appreciate it."

"Do it!" Ulian ordered. Erda initiated the top thrusters to slow them down, allowing all systems to catch up. Something whined deep within the ship, the sound of the dampeners settling back to normal operation. Once the pressure alleviated, it became easier to breathe and sit up straight.

"Why is it holding together?" Morala asked. "You can see the breaks throughout the ship. It should be in pieces."

"Oh my ..." Viran sighed. "Quite clever. They've rigged their shield generators, their reactor, everything has become magnetic. The whole ship is held together by it. That's why it's still in one piece despite the bombs. The crew must've done it when they decided to ram us. They knew we'd hit them with everything we had."

Ulian's shoulders ached but he ignored the pain, staring at the screen. "Where's that thing going to crash down?"

"Calculating," Viran said. "The northern continent, roughly six thousand kilometers away from the base." Pretty far."

"Damage potential?" Morala asked.

Viran whistled. "Catastrophic. The reactor hasn't gone off yet. If it does within the atmosphere, it would be like dropping dirty bombs to the order of … six in one spot. Though the destruction would be immediate with only minor lingering side effects. Easily cleaned up by an environmental team."

"Time to impact?" Ulian asked.

"Twenty-five minutes at the current speed."

The ship shook again from another attack by the destroyers. "Those annoying gnats," Morala muttered. "Erda, target those bastards and light them up."

Ulian leaned close to her, lowering his voice, "do you think we should try to annihilate that ship? Prevent it from hitting the planet?"

"I suppose that depends on whether it's possible to do so," Morala said. "Considering what Viran described, we might knock some pieces off but we practically need to ram into them to divert their course. Besides, how bad can the impact be? A few tremors? Nothing that should prevent the ground troops from finishing their mission."

"Shuttle traffic may be impossible," Viran said. "Sorry to eavesdrop … but the immediate effects will involve a dramatic, natural response. Basically, horrible storms."

"Ah." Morala cleared her throat. "We can try, but our bombs didn't do the trick. We could chase the thing over there … let the Gnosis deal with the destroyers."

"Get me Captain Bradford," Ulian said. "I'll pose the question to him."

***

Desmond held his seat as Zach brought them in for their attack run on Trall's ship, watching the screen intently as they unleashed everything they had on the ship. It caused considerable damage but not enough to bring it down. That was to be expected. They charged up for a second go when the Stalwart peppered the enemy with missiles.

The projectiles caused such a flash when they hit, Desmond felt dazzled. He rubbed his eyes, squinting to see what had happened. Orange lines decorated the surface, fire bulging the hull. The Stalwart popped upward, a dramatic and swift motion that took them well above Trall's ship as it sailed by.

"That thing is done," Salina said. "All systems are down."

"Why's it not blowing up then?" Vincent asked.

"Some kind of magnetic pull at the center is holding the ship together," Salina replied. "Something extremely powerful but they are effectively dead. It's a big ballistic missile at this point."

"Captain!" Zach pointed. "Incoming enemy destroyer."

"Lock on and open fire," Desmond said. "Evasive maneuvers."

The ship darted again, this time tossing Desmond left in his seat. He grunted from the suddenness of the motion, clinging hard to his arm rests. Their weapons fired, half striking their target. Before the enemy could shoot at them, Zach initiated their primary thrusters. They darted away from their former position, moving into a new firing solution.

"Stalwart on the line," Salina said.

"Send it over here." Desmond gestured to his station. "Ulian, what's going on?"

"Trall's ship is dead," Ulian replied, "but it can still cause a lot of trouble. We've plotted its course. It will crash on the planet's surface. The damage will be catastrophic, including a storm which may delay departure for some time … possibly worse."

"We're reading some kind of magnetics. What do you propose we do to stop it?"

"We have twenty-five minutes to hit it with everything we've got, to knock pieces off at the very least to minimize the damage to the planet." Ulian shrugged. "I think that's the only choice at this point."

"What is up with these maniacs and their attempts to crash into planets?" Desmond grumbled. "I say we finish these destroyers then focus everything on the battleship. Agreed?"

Ulian nodded. "Indeed. You've got yours, we'll finish the other one. Ulian out."

"Keep hitting them, Zach," Desmond said. "Once again, we're on a crazy timeline. This one might not be as bad as back home but I'd rather not have a whole lot of people stranded down there for any longer than they have to be."

Chapter 10

Heat disembarked the shuttle, following Fielding and Dashwood as they burst onto the field. Once they cleared their ship, each of them initiated their jump packs, carrying them a few hundred yards from their landing zone. As they landed amongst the rocks nearby, enemy fire chased them, energy beams splashing against rocks and winking into the sky.

The shuttles performed a quick pass over the area, bombarding the heaviest resistance. Heat saw pieces of enemies scattered about the area, arms and legs tossed from the impact points. As he came down in his cover, he darted to the edge of the massive boulder, using his HUD to get a zoomed view of their destination.

Double doors were wide open, offering easy access to the base. Cassie's data showed the Orbs were in there, somewhere off to the left. He had a waypoint to follow to get there, though the exact path would likely be complicated by hallways. The facility itself was not as large as he anticipated but according to scans, there were other structures nearby.

Other barracks for the men we killed back on Earth. Heat took aim and fired at one of the half walls the enemy used for cover. His attack struck the surface, proving it was sturdy enough not to move from a quick hit. He initiated his jump pack, launching himself high enough to see over it.

One soldier crouched there, practically cowering. He peppered him with multiple shots, tearing through his personal shield and ending him a moment later. *Shit, where were those shields on Earth? They didn't have them! These guys must've exhausted their resources, depleted their supplies.*

Heat landed and charged for the door. "I'm going in," he spoke over the com. "Gillet, you with me?"

"A little busy!" Gillet shouted.

Heat looked around, saw heavier enemy resistance on the opposite side of his position. He redirected, laying into the cluster of Tol'An soldiers from behind. He counted six total men and he took down three in a second. One spun and fired back, a clean miss. He was rewarded with a blow from behind right in the head.

Another group charged out from beside the building, causing Heat to hit his jump pack again. Their combined attack caught the ground where he'd been standing a moment before. He landed on the roof, dropping low to avoid additional fire.

Rockets exploded. Weapons fire filled the air. The Pahxin soldiers came upon them, slicing through the enemy ranks. Heat peeked over the side and noted he had a clean line of sight to the base. "We've got to get in there!" He shouted. "We can secure the Orbs while they take care of the rest!"

"Where is everyone?" Fielding asked. He landed near the door and Heat joined him. "That's one. Dashwood? Where are you?"

"We're engaged," Dashwood said. "The Rat and I are a little busy."

Gillet joined them at the door.

"Okay, help the Pahxin," Fielding said. "We're going in. Wish us luck." He waved for the others to follow him. "I'm on point. Let's go."

Heat followed the lieutenant into the facility, pausing immediately as something to the right caught his eye. "Sir," he said. "Hold on." He moved over and found two bodies lying on the ground, ghastly wounds decorating their throats. "None of us did this. Someone knifed these two."

"Creepy," Fielding said. "I'm guessing someone turned on them."

"Then hid the bodies?" Heat asked. "Something about this doesn't feel right."

"We don't have time to worry about it now." Fielding patted him on the shoulder. "Come on, we have to move. I've got the waypoint. Follow me."

Heat cast a lingering glance at the bodies before complying. He didn't like the look of it but if there was a knife wielding maniac running around, at least it wouldn't matter to them. The guy wasn't about to pierce the power armor with an edged weapon. That didn't mean he couldn't cause some other kind of trouble.

Like detonating the Orbs.

***

Gizan passed through the living quarters, moving slower. A man burst around the corner, a technician carrying a gun. They made eye contact for a brief moment before the newcomer bowed his head in deference. The barrel of his weapon dropped toward the floor as he did.

"My Lord, you've come back. Thank all that is holy."

"Yes." Gizan continued walking. "I'm here to make it all right."

"How bad is it?"

"Bad." Gizan lashed out, slicing the man's throat. The tech's eyes went wide as he dropped his weapon, grasping at the wound. Dropping to the floor, he gurgled out his final moments. "But only for a certain few."

The Trindishas were not far off, just a room away. He approached Ezria's chamber, paused to look at where the devices were held. Such an inordinate amount of power there. He shook his head. The Tol'An were not mature enough to wield such wonders. They didn't deserve what they had.

Gizan tapped the panel, stepping into the large, mostly empty room overlooking the sea. The lights were out, only the sunlight illuminated the dim space. He'd been there several times. Taken missions from the man who called himself a master. The rest chambers were to the left beside the washroom.

"Come out!" Gizan shouted. "Do not make me come hunting you down like a terrified animal. I think we've all sacrificed enough honor for cowardice."

Ezria stepped into the room from the rest chambers, carrying a knife. He was naked from the waist up, scars decorating his muscular body. Black, loose fitting trousers ended in bare feet. His eyes carried a glint of madness as he stepped forward, smiling with a chilling, rictus grin.

"I've been hunting you," Ezria said. "Across the stars."

"Yes, well. Here I am." Gizan tilted his head. He tossed the rifle aside. "Do you think you can stand against me with a blade?"

"I intend to try," Ezria replied. "Before I followed Calatha, I fought in the slave pits of Alava Nine. Illegal ... possibly run by the Kalrawv Group but who could prove it?" He shook his head. "I can fight, Gizan. I just had tools to do the work for me. Such as you. My finest weapon ... dulled and eventually turned on me."

"Perhaps if you hadn't imprisoned me for a single failure, things would've been different."

"You think I should've been easy on you?"

"Military operations are not guarantees and people deserve second chances."

"That is where you are wrong. You've proven that. Once failure takes hold, a soul is lost forever."

"Enough of this!" Gizan spit on the floor. "You ruined the ideals of the Tol'An. You tread upon the honor of Calatha and you have betrayed the very reason this organization was formed. I am ending your life right now. Today, your incompetent reign ends and with it, the organization you corrupted."

Gizan dashed forward, wielding his knives backward in his hands. He swiped at Ezria's face but the man faded away, dancing as a flurry of blows nearly gutted him. But the former master remained unscathed, bouncing on the balls of his feet.

Initiating another swift array of attacks, Gizan put everything he had into the assault. Ezria once again evaded them, keeping just out of range. His agility shocked the assassin, especially considering he'd never seen him perform such moves before.

Who trained this man? Gizan thought. *He's far better than I would've given him credit for!*

Just as Gizan decided to commit to another attack, Ezria hopped forward, landing a thrust kick to Gizan's stomach. The blow shocked him, knocking him backward and forcing him to take a knee. The wind rushed from his lungs and he fought to breathe. Holding his weapon up defensively, he fought to recover.

Ezria advanced again, throwing a kick for Gizan's face. The assassin rolled out of the way, swiping his knife as he did. He felt it find resistance and pass through, slicing through Ezria's pants and cutting him just above the knee.

The man hissed in response then threw himself at Gizan, attacking like a feral animal. They blocked and struck, advanced and fell back. Each cut the other, superficial wounds on the forearms and hands. Something stung just below Gizan's left eye as hot blood covered his cheek. He lashed out with a kick, connecting with Ezria's groin.

They both fell out of range, panting and gasping. "You are good," Ezria said. "I have definitely not lost your edge."

"None of this matters," Gizan said. "The humans are here. The Pahxin. They'll execute you even if I do not."

"And they will martyr me!"

"No one cares about you enough to find your death particularly compelling." Gizan attacked again, launching himself at Ezria. He led held one knife back while leading with the other. Ezria stood at the last second, allowing the leading blade to sink into his shoulder. They both fell to the ground.

Gizan gasped as terrible pain rushed through his midsection. He plunged his free weapon into the side of Ezria's neck, making the man's eyes go wide and mouth pop open. He sawed twice until he felt bone, blood spraying from a severed artery. Nothing would save Ezria after that.

"It's over now." Gizan tried to rise but the pain in his stomach made it difficult. He looked down. The handle of Ezria's weapon stuck out of him, the blade deep in his midsection. Moving caused so much agony, he nearly fell unconscious. He stumbled to the wall, leaning against it.

Ezria sputtered and hissed, pressing at his wound. He began to convulse, legs kicking feebly before he finally went still. His last breath came as a wheeze, signaling not only his end but that of the Tol'An as an effective force. The ones fighting above didn't know they were done, but it was just a matter of time.

Heavy footfalls sounded from down the way, the familiar sound of human power armor. Gizan couldn't help but smile. To have found success only to be killed by a lesser race, one that barely learned how to travel the stars ... it struck him as humorous. And perhaps a little unfair.

"Gizan!" Rythi's voice exploded over his com. "Come in!"

"I'm here," Gizan muttered. Anything louder hurt too much. "What is it?"

"Something's going to crash on the planet! Something really big! We have minutes ... eighteen to twenty at the most! We have to get out of here!"

"You go," Gizan replied. "I'm sorry that I could not reward you for your efforts. You deserved to get something for this."

"I'm not leaving without you!"

"I do not believe I will survive for much longer," Gizan said. "I've completed the task but the enemy approaches ... and I've been terribly wounded. Save yourself ... friend. I'm ... done."

Rythi was silent for several moments. "I'm sorry. I know you wanted to have a normal life in the end. Rest well ... wherever you end up."

"You as well." Gizan turned off the com and slumped to the ground. He stared out the window. He couldn't see the waves from his vantage point but the horizon was clearly visible. He smiled at the view. It would look quite different after whatever hit the planet that worried Rythi but he doubted he'd be alive to see it.

Just as well, Gizan thought. *I've done what I set out to do. I've atoned. I deserve nothing more than this death. Die as one lives … that … has always been … the way.* He swallowed hard. Most of his body went numb. Blood soaked his pants. He forced himself to remain awake, to stare at the water. If he could choose his final sight, it would be that.

***

"Right down here!" Fielding shouted. He stopped dead in his tracks. Gillet ran into him. "Slow down guys. Look at this body."

Heat stepped forward. Another man had his throat cut. "This is the work of someone who really did turn on them. Jesus."

"Hold on." Fielding pressed his hand against his helmet. He paced away. "Shit, guys. I just got word that battleship might hit the planet. The Gnosis and Stalwart are trying to blow it up but they might not pull it off. We have to secure the payloads and get them out of here immediately."

They hustled down the hall, pausing at the final two doors. "It's one of these," Fielding said. "Gillet, you and Heat grab that one on the left. I'll do the right."

Heat tapped the panel and stepped inside. His eyes fell on a body lying in a pool of blood, hands pressed at a gaping wound on the throat. It was naked from the waist up, covered in gore and scars. *Who the hell is that guy?* He wondered. *He can't be the leader of the Tol'An ... can he?*

"Look," Gillet said. "Remember this guy?"

Heat turned and gazed down at another man, barely breathing. A knife stuck out of his gut, tiny cuts marred his face and arms. He looked terrible. "Holy shit. Yeah. He attacked Cassie that time. He was wanted by the Pahxin big time. So he turned on the Tol'An, huh?" He initiated the speaker to talk outside the suit. "You still alive?"

"For the present." The man rasped. He didn't take his eyes off the window.

"Who was that you killed?"

"Ezria Tolva ... farcical ruler of the Tol'An."

"I was right," Heat muttered. "I thought as much. Why'd you kill him?"

"He was a fool ... a traitor to the cause ... a monster."

"Like you were much better," Gillet said.

"And I am suffering for it."

Heat nodded. "Probably true."

"Think we could save him?" Gillet asked.

Heat huffed. "What for? To be executed? Let him bleed out here." He knelt beside him. "You caused a lot of pain and suffering. You were there when you kidnapped our ambassador and you tried to destroy society." He gripped the knife. "I hope it's hot wherever you end up." He yanked the blade free, drawing a gurgled cry from the man.

Blood gushed from the wound. The Tol'An man breathed heavily several times before sliding down to his side. He died a moment later. Heat dropped the knife on his body. "Come on. Fielding probably has the Orbs. And whatever this was ... it's over. This lot got what they deserved in a major way. Justice was swift for once ... and bloody."

***

Cassie stared at her screen, tapping her foot as she waited for a report. The marines were in position, they'd entered the building. It wasn't that large. The Tol'An seemed to spread out, turning the area into a small town for lodging and storage. The main complex housed a nominal defense, but it was falling rapidly.

Salina let them know that the battleship was on the way. They tried to hurry but there was only so much they could do. Of course, they knew exactly where to go. The only obstacles to gathering the devices might've been additional soldiers within the facility but she had a feeling they would commit all their defenses to repel the invading force.

Fielding reached out to her a few minutes later. "We've secured the Orbs," he said. She breathed a sigh of relief. "Heat found a dead guy that you might remember. Some freak who attacked you at the mining facility?"

"Oh my … did you guys kill him?"

"Looks like some internal shit," Fielding said. "Pardon my language. He fought with what he claimed was the leader of the Tol'An. They're both dead. I informed the Pahxin. They'll probably come in to collect the bodies. Apparently, both of them are wanted. Anyway, we're coming out with the devices now. How much time before impact?"

Cassie leaned to look at Salina's screen. "Twelve minutes. The Stalwart made short work of the destroyers ... still not sure what they were hoping to accomplish. The Tol'An was done. They could've made this easy on everyone."

"Not exactly the way of terrorists, ma'am," Fielding said. "We'll be back soon. Fielding out."

"They have the Orbs!" Cassie shouted. "They're bringing them out now!"

"Wonderful," Desmond said. "Now if we can destroy this battleship before it crashes into the planet, we might make for an easy trip back up to orbit for them. Zach, how close are we?"

"I'm firing now. The Stalwart is hitting them as well."

Salina turned. "The goal is to knock as many parts off as possible so that it doesn't go down whole."

"I got that," Zach grumbled. "But every time I hit it, the thing just has more holes. Small chunks get dislodged but the larger ones ... it's like the whole thing has been turned into a massive magnet. If that's the case, doesn't that mean it'll be impossible to dislodge it completely? We'd have to use cutting lasers to slice through it and that would take time."

"More than we've got," Desmond replied. "But we have to try. Keep at it."

Cassie turned to watch the view screen. Both ships brutalized the battleship, tearing large pieces off but not big enough to prevent it from causing serious damage. Her own screen started beeping. She turned back to those scans. The source of the planetary interference was leaving. It lifted off, heading for the opposite side of the planet.

Really! Who the hell are you? Cassie marked them. "Captain, I've got a departing ship from the surface."

"Don't have time now," Desmond said. "We're a little busy."

Salina announced, "on that note of not having time, I'm picking up a large hyperspace signature." She paused. "Oh! The Pahxin fleet! They're here! They've arrived."

"Zach!" Desmond called. "Come on, get it somewhere good!"

"I'm trying!" Zach fired again, searing off one of the thrusters. It tumbled away from the whole just as the Stalwart lit up the side. Finally, the ship began to break up, cast into far more manageable chunks. Cassie stood, staring at the debris they created. It had been caught by the gravitational pull of the planet—it was definitely going down.

But now, there were *many* pieces. Cassie did some calculations. The damage from many of them wouldn't be too bad but the largest chunks would devastate the regions they landed in. As they began to streak into the atmosphere, turning into fiery shards, Salina cleared her throat.

"Good news, bad news," Salina said. "Good: we're not going to see a world ending event or anything. The bad: some of those chunks are going to hit hard near the facility now and when they do, it's going to be like someone carpet bombed the area. Estimated time to impact: four minutes."

"Where are they with the Orbs?" Vincent asked. "Are they on the shuttles yet?"

Cassie reached out to Fielding with the news, feeling the urgency as she initiated the contact. She held her breath as the line began to beep ...

***

Heat shoved one of the Orbs into the first shuttle, stepping back. Gillet took the other one, hefting it toward their other means off the planet. He leaned against the ship, casting a gaze around the area to see if any other fighting was going on. The Pahxin had rounded up several prisoners, a couple dashed inside to gather the rest.

They'd leave with thirty-five men, some soldiers, others techs and of course the two bodies they were so desperate for. All those got loaded up in one of the shuttles. Chances were good they couldn't occupy the area, especially with the battleship coming down. Heat directed his gaze up, eyes widening.

Streaks of fire seemed to be coming in their direction. He anticipated seeing *something* but that ... took him by surprise.

"We've got problems!" Fielding shouted. "Launch! Launch! Get the Orbs out of here!"

The two shuttles throttled up and departed, flying rapidly away from the base. That left one shuttle to get *all* the marines out of there. The Pahxin ships were full and even if they crammed them all together, the final shuttle couldn't carry all of them. Weight restrictions meant at least two, probably three would have to stay behind.

"You guys go," Fielding said. "Get on the shuttle. Dashwood and I will figure it out."

"Begging your pardon," Heat said, "but there's no way I'm letting two lieutenants stick it out down here. Vine, get your ass off that shuttle. Gillet, come with me."

"What're you doing?" Fielding grabbed his arm. "Those pieces are going to land here soon! You have to go!"

"Get on the shuttle, sir." Heat pointed. "We're going to have to rocket our asses out of here if we want to survive and we don't have time to argue." He turned to the others. "Follow me, I have an idea."

"You're a crazy son of a bitch, Heat!" Fielding nodded to Dashwood and the two men boarded the shuttle. It lifted off a moment later.

Heat gestured for them to follow him as he initiated his jump pack, hurling himself toward the building. He landed on the roof, the other two close behind. The sound of the chunks approaching, a heavy whistling sound started to build. He didn't risk a look, just turned his attention to the water and jumped again.

They sailed through the air, reaching an apex as the first of the chunks slammed into the ground with a deafening impact. Their helmets protected them but shockwave sent them an additional two hundred yards out toward the sea. Heat looked down as the water approached. His legs entered first, causing a tremendous splash as he sank into the depths.

The rest of the chunks pummeled the base, a couple striking the sea some distance off. Heat watched them on his scans as he used his rockets to remain close to the surface. Two minutes of constant barrage shook the area before all of them ended. The biggest pieces would hit farther away to the north.

"You still alive?" Fielding called into the com. "Can you hear me?"

"We're underwater," Gillet said. "Heat led us into the sea."

"Nicely played. We achieved orbit and we'll send someone back for you ASAP. Can you get to the surface?"

"Yeah, why not?" Heat muttered. "It wouldn't be a mission if we weren't in some inconvenient place at the end. We'll see you soon, sir. Thanks for not trying to order me back onto the shuttle."

"I doubt you would've listened."

"That's why I'm thanking you. I've been through too much to have a court martial finish it off."

Epilogue

"They got them!" Cassie shouted. "The Orbs are on their way back to the Gnosis! Injuries only, no deaths!"

"Thank God." Desmond rubbed his eyes. "The real fight was back home. This ... this was a brawl."

"Ulian's on the line," Salina added. "He's congratulating us on the operation. The fleet's incoming to help mop up. With the interference gone, I've found the other pockets of Tol'An. They're all over the southern continent ... far enough away from the crashing spaceship to survive."

"Well, the fleet can handle that," Desmond replied. "I think we're going to secure our people and get ready to go home. I think everyone would like to see what happens when you put six orbs in a room. Complete the collection and what happens next?"

I'm not so excited, Cassie thought. She knew the technicians back at the base, the AIA and Doctor Harper, Thayne and the Pahxin all had experiments they wanted to run. None of them sounded fun to her. All she wanted was some time off ... and maybe to never see an Orb in person again.

"Why do you think they threw everything at Earth?" Vincent asked. "What was the point?"

"They were relying on allies to help them," Desmond replied. "If the militia would've hit again just at the same time, with that traitor unimpeded, God knows how bad that could've gone. AIA caught him just in time. Who knows how much damage he could've caused? But when they saw that they weren't going to steal the Orbs, they tried to blow them up."

"It seems to me," Salina said, "that maybe they thought we hadn't figured out where their base was. By taking them out, we never would've learned about this place."

"True." Desmond nodded. "And then, they could keep flourishing. The gamble didn't pay off, but I understand it. Their ambush caught us off guard. Men and women weren't in position for the fight. We pulled it off, but not without some losses. Before we left, I heard some of our smaller ships, the old experimental ones that were refitted? They took heavy casualties."

"Pahxin destroyers were taken out," Cassie said. "And a large number of fighters. One of the battleships also is disabled and will require extensive repair. A Captain ... Torqua's ship actually. Over sixty ground forces that weren't in power armor died and we lost civilians too. The numbers weren't tallied before we left."

"So no joke," Desmond said. "Witness history, ladies and gentlemen. The end of a terrorist organization plaguing the galaxy for years. We were a part of that. And now, we can finally look toward peace. Not just for us, but for the colonies and other places these guys hit and assaulted. The people they kidnapped and murdered … all avenged."

"Works for me." Vincent leaned back in his chair. "I'm telling you, I'm exhausted. Think we can avoid a fight for like … two weeks or something? Maybe we can take the slow hyperspace lane back. Buy ourselves a couple days. We can make up a story about bad navigation routes."

"I'm not taking that hit," Zach replied with a chuckle.

"We'll have time for rest now," Desmond said. "And a whole lot of other things as well. Thank you all. Let's secure our people, talk to the fleet and get the hell out of here. Earth's going to want the good news and I'm pretty sure everyone on board would like a chance to celebrate. I know we've *all* earned it."